CLEAN UP
ON
AISLE THREE

JORDAN O'HALLORAN

Dedicated to the man with the yellow pants and blue eyes, I miss you every day, grandpa. Thanks for always believing in me.

And, to anyone who has supported me in this journey by reading this book, thank you. This book is proof of a dream made true because of you.

CHAPTER ONE

My mom says she found out about me in a graffiti filled, urine-smelling truck stop bathroom. She was sixteen, hadn't had her period in over two months and craved nothing but gummy worms and stale tortilla chips.

My grandpa chased her out of the house the day after she peed on that white stick. She said my grandpa doesn't believe in God. But that day, in Arizona, I'm sure he did. He claimed my mom had the devil enter her between her legs, and what would arrive those quick seven months later was sure to be the worst mistake of her life.

So, hello. Nice to meet you. I'm that mistake. But you can call me Lucy. Born and raised here in the Sonoran Desert and I always pray for rain.

Mom and I live with her boyfriend, Chuck Williams. She says my SS—sperm supplier—moved to Michigan right after I was born. The only time I met the guy was way before I can even remember. There are a few pictures of him. In an old shoebox somewhere in the attic, they're getting pretty faded now. It kind of sucks at times knowing I'll never know my *dad*, but I guess it could be worse. He could be a total creep or something.

Chuck always wears the same old red-and-green flannel shirt on his days off, has toothpaste stuck in his messy and going-gray beard, and fills the fridge with silver and red half-empty beers he swears he'll finish. If having six or more beer cans in the fridge with a few sips taken out of each was an Olympic event, Chuck would win the gold every time. Mom's also an alcoholic, so him taking a few sips is his subtle way of making her stop drinking. Sadly, it hasn't worked yet.

Despite Chuck's complete dorkiness, he's still pretty cool. He gave me a job at his family grocery store, Smiles. Smiles is owned by his filthy-rich, conspiracy theory filled dad, Raymond. Chuck's the manager. He hired me to help me save money. I hate the job, but it's work experience, so I guess I should be grateful.

The only thing that gets me through each day is knowing that after graduation, I'm getting out of Arizona. I can't wait to leave. My boyfriend, Ben, and I have plans to move to Seattle. It's not like anything's keeping me here. I don't have a whole bunch of friends or even family.

Ben and I have been inseparable since we were in 3rd grade. I can't say when we got together because I don't even remember. I think one day we held hands and decided that we liked the way it felt.

Ben is 6'3 which makes him exactly a foot taller than me. He inherited his dad's thick, red, flowing hair that reaches his shoulders. He's obsessed with Pez dispensers and loves peanut butter. Ben was diagnosed with Autism at 6 years old when our teacher noticed he organized everything in the classroom by color. Including everyone's backpacks. The Autism thing is pretty cool because he's my own personal encyclopedia, thesaurus, and atlas all in one adorable package. I'm lucky.

Right now, I'm getting dressed for work in my dumb work shirt. Since the store is called Smiles, the work shirts are bright yellow with a cartoon smiley face on it. It's embarrassing. I work in the meat department, which sucks because I've been a vegetarian for almost five years. Chuck knows this, but he and my mom like to punish me for what they call my, *bad* attitude. Though that attitude is honestly caused by them ninety-nine percent of the time.

There are kids at my school who do drugs, get tattoos, and brag about getting alcohol poisoning. But I left the house at 2 a.m. one time to rescue a stray cat and according to Mom and Chuck I'm the worst teenager in all of Arizona.

"Lucy, you almost ready to go?" Chuck shouts through my purple door. "We're gonna be late! I have a lot of work today."

"I'll be right there," I yell over my Glitter Tooth playlist on my phone. I'm putting on my vanilla-scented deodorant, taking my chalky tasting pills with lukewarm water, then I run out of my room like a lightning bolt.

Mom never cleans after herself. The kitchen's full of cereal bowls with rotten milk, spoons stuck to the sides, and empty water bottles.

Chuck's already there drinking his black coffee over the sink. He hates creamer. Coffee on its own is gross if you ask me.

He says, "Let's get out of here. Ready for donuts?"

"Yeah. But I want to say goodbye to Mom really quick. Is she still sleeping or something?"

"I don't know where she is. She didn't come home last night. Maybe she spent the night at someone's house after the bars."

Chuck and I are used to mom not coming back after the bars. She usually meets up with one of her friends and she ends up passing out at their house. I wish she didn't have to drink so much, and I've tried helping her stop. Nothing ever sticks. It's so annoying, but at least she doesn't have a DUI or something.

"Good point. Oh well, we'll see her later." I lock the dark blue door behind.

Chuck starts up his black truck, Bruce. He doesn't allow anyone to drive it, especially Mom. I swear the thing is the baby he never had. Bruce is always spotless. I mean, normal people don't wash their cars every Friday night, right? Because that is part of Chuck's routine. The only exception to Bruce staying spotless, with Chuck's No Eating rule is every Sunday when we enjoy powdered donuts together on the way to work.

We ride down desert roads full of green cacti and brown sand. The sun's blinding me and I'm already too warm. I'm looking forward to escaping this heat. I need to get out of here and away from the same people I've known since kindergarten.

As the truck engine rumbles, Chuck asks, "You doing okay, Lucy? Noticed you were up late last night."

"Yeah, I'm fine. I was watching a movie and writing some poems."

"Oh, okay. It was loud in there. The sound echoed through the hallway. You going to let me hear your poems one of these days? I'd like to."

"I'll read you one later. I'm still tired. I don't know if you realize this or not, but it's 7 a.m. on a Sunday. You didn't even have Ben come in today. Not cool, dude."

"Hey, you're getting paid for working! You should feel grateful about that. And today we're getting our donuts and chocolate milk, remember?"

I roll my eyes because he's right. Powdered donuts and chocolate milk are the ways to my heart. It's our tradition every week; only the two of us know about.

I guess I could try being more grateful, but my newly diagnosed bipolar disorder is seriously making me feel even more insane. I can barely keep my thoughts straight. My brain doesn't let me sleep, and it seems like every other minute, my mood changes.

As we pull into the corner Lucky Liquor, I find myself full of panic. I'm not sure what that's even about, but I'm going to try and take some deep breaths. I always have panic these days. I'm not sure what causes it most of the time, and that makes it extra frustrating.

Lucky Liquor is owned by this guy named Miguel who always gives Smiles business. He's been friends with Chuck since they were kids and the two of them are like brothers. Miguel comes into Smiles for groceries, and Chuck comes here for donuts, cigarettes, and beer. Seems like a pretty good exchange if you ask me.

The bell jingles as I walk in. I head straight for the fridge full of chocolate milk and energy drinks. Don't worry, I'm not drinking the two together. I'm not a monster. The milk is for my donuts and the energy drink is the fuel I'm going to need to make it through my shift today.

Miguel asks, "Hey, Lucy! How's your mom?"

I hate that everyone asks me that. Everyone in this stupid town knows her. She's well-known for being the girl who had a baby when she was in high school. I mean, she's thirty-three with a seventeen-year-old daughter. I wouldn't say that's entirely the path everyone takes. This town is full of gun-lovers, Bible-quoting grandmas, which means teen pregnancy is shunned here. It doesn't help that mom still dresses like a seventeen-year-old.

I put my stuff on the counter. "She's fine. I'll tell her you said hi."

"Two packs of Golden Gaucho cigarettes, please," Chuck asks. "Luce, did you get me donuts too?"

"Of course. How could I forget?" I jiggle his powdered donuts. Chuck swipes his card and I open my donuts. I'm starving.

"Couldn't wait, Lucy?" Miguel laughs.

My mouth's too full to respond, so I shake my head and try swallowing faster. "See you later, dude!" I tell Miguel, then I head out to the car.

We drive to Smiles and I'm already ready to go home. The red sign isn't lit up yet and the parking lot is empty. The way I like it. The two of us weave through the lot and go in from the back, since it's easier to open the store this way.

Raymond's car is already here. He's the absolute worst. He'll sometimes help on Sundays since it's our busiest day of the week. He'll tell Chuck he "just wants to make sure everything's running smoothly", but I'm pretty sure he's being a control freak.

I roll my eyes, "Are you serious? He's here? Why didn't you tell me?"

Chuck shakes his head, "Lucy, calm down. I didn't know either. Don't get mad. He's probably here to help. The store is going to be super busy today."

"Whatever. I'm not going to be nice, though. He's been such a weirdo to me lately. I regret showing him how to watch videos on his phone."

"Why? What's he doing now?"

"He's been showing me some insane videos. He's trying to make me believe all of these conspiracy theories with him."

"Seriously?"

"Yep. He told me yesterday that all politicians are lizards who are performing mind control on humans. Apparently, the lizards are planning an uprising to get rid of all humans."

"Wow. I told him to stop that. It's worse than I thought. He's scaring customers away. Tune him out if you can."

"I'll try…"

I don't tell Chuck this, but Raymond's also been telling me how robots are going to start taking everyone's jobs. He said that in the next ten years, Smiles is going to have robots stock the shelves. On top of his stupid theories, he won't even let homeless people use the bathroom. He also cheats on his wife, with the produce manager here at the store. Everyone, including the customers, know about it, so they're not as sneaky as they think.

I feel like my life's one cruel joke after another. I hate being bipolar. I hate having to be in Arizona. I hate this grocery store.

I should get rid of this bad attitude because I'm going to be stuck here for the next eight hours.

With my therapist's guidance, I have a new mantra I say to myself, *'My bipolar doesn't define me.'* It's especially helpful in moments like these. Lost and consumed by this disease.

My bipolar doesn't define me.

My bipolar doesn't define me.

I got this.

As I wash my hands with the pink soap that dries them out, Chuck screams, "Lucy, call the police. Right now!"

"What's going on?"

"No time for questions. Call them!"

I don't know what to do. I grab my orange phone out of my apron pocket and with shaky hands dial nine-one-one.

The operator asks, "What's your emergency?"

I feel like there's a bowling ball stuck in my throat. "Hi... this is Lucy. Lucy McBride. Can you please come to Seventh and Camden to the Smiles Grocery Store?"

"I'll need more details to assist you, little girl."

I cover the phone, so the lady doesn't hear me yelling. "What's going on? I need to tell the police something to make them come there."

"My dad's dead, Lucy. Someone... Someone murdered him." Chuck's crying.

Choking on words, I say, "Hi, uh, sorry. There's been a murder at the store and we need help. I don't know any more details." My heart pounds through my ears. I'm definitely having a heart attack.

"Okay, are you safe? Is there someone there? To help you?" The nice lady on the other end replies.

"I'm safe. I think My mom's boyfr-he's crying a lot. Found his dad. I'm here in the back of the store. Don't know more details, I think I'll be okay."

"Okay, it's going to be all right. I'll send someone right now. Stay safe. Say hi to your mom for me!"

Is she fucking serious? Can she even say that? I hang up before the operator asks me any more questions and walk out of my meat department bubble. I see it. A long trail of blood, like a large snake slithered through the once white aisle.

I hear Chuck choking out his words, "Why?" and "What the fuck, Dad?"

I can't believe what I'm seeing. Chuck's a hunched over mess in aisle three. Aisle three— that's the middle of the produce what is the current term for bipolar department. All the yellow, green, and pink-fleshed apples are now covered in Raymond's blood.

A part of me wants to add humor to the situation, say, '*Clean Up on Aisle Three*!' But, that's definitely insensitive. Even for me.

I'm too scared to look past the blood-stricken apples to see Ray's dead body. I've never seen one except in the horror movies Ben and I watch. The difference is that movie bodies are fake. This is the remains of a once breathing, talking asshole who walked around these aisles all the time.

My curiosity gets the best of me. Shit. He has two bullets in his chest and has a look of shock on his face. I mean, I'd be shocked too if I was killed in a Smiles. But, the fact that this was *his* Smiles was probably heartbreaking. He fell among these fluorescent aisled walls with the waxed-coated apples.

I should've never looked. I feel bad for the guy. My heart feels like it's about to explode out of my body and join Raymond on the floor.

As my vision blurs and the vibrant lights burn my eyes, everything is swirling into one. The walls are starting to close in. My chest's heavy. I can't breathe right. I want Ben or my mom to come and save me. But Ben might not answer my text I sent after the 911 call, and Mom's probably hungover. Just my luck.

Before I can even take a full breath, I hear sirens in the parking lot. The howling noise makes the hair stand up on my arms and I get shivers from my arms to my toes. My body feels tense, almost as if I'm flexing like a bodybuilder. Everything spins. I can't focus on any one item in the store; they're blended together. Why do all the green vegetables look exactly the same? Such a pretty shade of forest green…

"Lucy. Lucy, wake up," Ben says, rubbing my sweaty hair.

I rub my eyes. "Where are we?" As I look around, there's police officers here, but I don't recognize them. Detective Mick Kane is talking to the other officers. Their voices sound like gibberish.

"We're in the break room. You passed out a while ago." Ben smiles. I've never been so happy to see someone in my life. His dimples and gap between his two teeth feel like home.

I pull off my apron immediately. It has blood on it from the ground meat. That smell is enough to make me pass out again. It's horrible. A reminder of Raymond's tragic fate. I can't believe I actually feel bad for him.

Where's Chuck? Did he pass out too? Is Raymond's body gone? I'm glad Ben's here with me now. I hope Mom's here somewhere too. She needs to know what's going on if she doesn't already. I mean, she's pretty disconnected from everything for the most part, but this is a pretty big deal.

Mick Kane, the only detective in town, comes over to the white couch. I know Mick because of all the times I've picked Mom up from the bars. Mick and his husband, Frank, own a bar in town called The Dirty Sailor. Mom's favorite.

Mick's pulled out his white notepad. "Hey, Lucy, how are you feeling?"

"Um, I was in aisle three, saw a very dead Raymond, No I'm in here. I'm a little confused and my head hurts. Everything after Raymond is a huge blur, though. Is Chuck okay? Is my mom here?"

Ben hands me a clear plastic cup, water from the cooler. "Lucy, slow down. One thing at a time. Drink this."

Mick says, "Chuck's gone. We took him down to the police station. Your mom's phone is going to voicemail. I have some questions to ask. You're going to need to come down to the station too."

"Are you for real?" I say while seeing blood oozing from Raymond's head every time I blink. "Do you think I killed Raymond or something? Wasn't my passing out from all that blood a big clue it wasn't me?" I don't do well with blood and guns freak me out.

"Lucy, let's go down to the station. I'll ask my questions. I'd like to keep investigating this case. It's protocol. We check with everyone who works here and is affiliated with the store. That includes you. Afraid of blood or not."

"Um, rude," Ben says. "Take it easy. We understand you're busy, but no reason to be mean."

"Sorry, I'm not trying to be rude. I need to ask everyone. It's part of my job."

"Does that clear it up?"

Turns out I'm not the killer, but we all knew that. Ben showed Mick his phone. In his phone was my panicked text from last night that prove my innocence.

"Yes, these messages are enough proof for me. I had to ask before we moved onto the next person. I don't want more people to be killed. We may have a killer on the loose and I'm not about to let that happen."

After that lengthy discussion with Mick, I feel defeated. The visions in my head keep going back to Raymond's dead body and lots of blood. His shocked face. I think going to aisle three one last time will make me have some closure. I want to heal from this as fast as possible.

Of all the times to be diagnosed bipolar, this happens. My meds were just starting to work, too. I'm probably going to need to double up on them. I know what you're thinking. *How insensitive.* Yeah, maybe. But, there's someone around here who thought it was okay to kill Raymond. Me, and my thoughts show I'm not *that* bad.

"Hey, monkey. What does *milf* mean?" Monkey's my mom's nickname for me. She's called me that for as long as I can remember.

"MILF? Mother I would like to fuck… Why?"

"Oh, some cute guys at the gas station today called me a MILF. I was going real quick to get Chuck and I some cigarettes. I think they said they went to your school. Do the names Mark and Aaron sound familiar to you?"

"No. But I'm definitely going to look for them next week. Maybe invite them over for dinner!" I say while winking.

"That's a great idea!" she pauses for a second. "Oh, you're making fun of me, aren't you?"

I nod. "Gotcha!"

I've already taken three days off from school. It may be close to graduation, but the idea of being around people right now sounds terrible. The store's going to be closed for a while. Chuck has been beyond sad. I wish I could help him, but I can't focus on anything except blood. I wish I could sleep and cry all day. I'm still taking my meds, but think I'll need a higher dose soon.

CHAPTER TWO

I've thought about reaching out to my best friends. They've texted me a few times. I'm way too sad to even maintain conversation.

"Lucy don't be such a drama queen. Not everyone can say they have a mom that's super-hot. I like it." She practices the sound of it again, "MILF. I can see it in sparkling lights now. Kelly McBride, MILF of the year!"

"How's Chuck doing? I haven't seen him. Hiding in your room?"

"Yeah, he's fine! I made him some coffee. He took a shower this morning. Making great progress. He even told me he liked my outfit before I went for our cigarettes. It'd be nice to get a compliment from you for once, too."

Is she for real? She's dressed like a 13-year-old. Why would I compliment that? I swear I feel like mom is my little sister 90% of the time. I love her because she's the only family I have. But sometimes I wish I had a more stable parent. Bet it would help me feel less crazy.

I roll my eyes, "You're so weird and embarrassing. Why's your skirt so short? I can see your leopard-print underwear. It that one of my tops?"

She looks at me as if it was the most obvious thing in the world, drawn-in eyebrows down and everything. "Yeah, I stole this shirt from your closet. Isn't it cute? I love sequins. It's not like you'll ever wear it again. Your belly would hang out anyway. I mean, if you lost thirty pounds, it'd look way better."

"Wow, had to go for the weight thing," I say, gulping hard. Her words feel like a punch in the stomach.

"I'm kidding. Don't be so serious all the time. You know I don't mean it, baby. You're beautiful, Monkey. The way you are. I'm so ready for tonight. I'm heading to the Dirty Sailor."

"What about Chuck? He is going with you?"

"No, he's staying home. I invited him a few times and he wants to be home. I need some girl time. He understands."

"I'm with Chuck. Home is the best place to be. Wait, don't you think the Dirty Sailor is the wrong place to go? I mean Mick is the detective on the case. Don't you think he'll be questioning you all night?"

"Don't worry. My alibi or whatever it's called checked out. He could never think bad about me anyway. I'm his best customer."

"How can you be his best customer? You never pay for your drinks."

Mom's always bragging about how they give her free vodka shots there. I didn't know free raspberry and blueberry alcohol was something to brag about until she told me.

"It's not my fault that people always want to buy me drinks. Besides, I deserve it. You're not always the easiest daughter to deal with. A lot of my gray hairs are from you."

"Uhh, thanks? What am I supposed to say back to that?"

"You know I'm kidding, baby girl. Anyway, I'm running late. Momma loves you." she says while her heels carry her to the door.

A part of me wants to yell at her for not being there for Chuck. She's always so selfish. But I have no energy to even brush my hair right now. Having a long conversation with someone who doesn't even want to change feels like a workout. She'll hopefully figure it out eventually.

Mom is also always craving validation and attention. The stupid thing is, she always tends to get it, but from the wrong type of people.

Before Mom introduced me to Chuck at Smiles when I was ten, we went through an amusement park of crazy people disguised as my mom's lovers. There was Tim, the clown who wasn't even funny and always smelled like rotten cheese. Gina, when my mom thought dating women would somehow solve her dating problems in general. She was wrong. Turns out women can be just as bad as men. I'll also never forget Jimmy. Jimmy was this guy from California who fit the stereotype of people from there. He called everyone dude and his hair was bleached blonde like he dyed it with sunscreen.

My favorite one of all the losers, before Chuck was in our lives, was this dude named Erik. He was the one who introduced me to vegetarianism and was the best cook. He always bought purple carrots, the greenest of broccoli, and yellow bell peppers in hopes of giving us what he called a more rainbow diet. My mom and I used to go to animal rights rallies with him. One time after one of those rallies, my mom took me to a fried chicken restaurant. Erik saw us there and broke up with her right in the restaurant. We never saw him again. I'll never understand why she chose to go to the one across the street from his house.

My mom's a magnet for idiots. We're bound to run into at least one anywhere we go. The creepy guys lurking everywhere around this town are always saying things like, "Oh, is that your sister?" or "How many years apart are you girls?" I always want to kick the creepy smiles off their dirty faces. Even at gas stations or when I pick her up from the bar when she's had too much. She tends to use vodka to escape her and Chuck's problems. Don't think it's solved one yet.

It doesn't help that she dresses younger than I do. For my birthday last year, a customer at the store got me a gift card to Teenage City. Teenage City is a store full of crop tops, high heels, and hoop earrings. I don't shop there, but my mom sure does. I gave her the gift card because she wouldn't stop bothering me about it. She came back the next day with the ugliest zebra-print heels I've ever seen in my life. She's a size ten but always buys a size seven since they make her feet look smaller. In the zebra-print shoes, though, her heels stuck out the whole time. It was hilarious, but only to me. Blisters aren't fun for anyone and as bad as it sounds, I laughed.

Sometimes, she always tells me I helped her grow up and to never make the same mistakes she did. I can't help but feel she means me, though. I don't ever want children. Ben knows this and agrees. The idea of another human sitting in my stomach for nine months and eating all my food is the most unappealing thing in the world. If anyone is going to eat all my food and take up my entire free time, I want it to be Ben or Snowball, the neighborhood stray cat I've adopted as my own.

The front door swings open while I'm reading my book from the library. Is mom home early? That's a first.

"Kelly, where are you, babe? I got us some orange chicken and chow mein. Your favorites!"

I look up at Chuck, from my time traveling cat book. "I thought you were in your room? Mom left to go to the bar. She said she invited you a few times."

"Yeah, she did. I'd rather be home. Since everyone knows about what happened, the idea of talking to people sounds like torture."

"I get it 100%. I'm sure she brought her phone if you need to talk to her."

"I need her right now. I hate that she keeps drinking. I'm debating going down there and stealing her away. What do you think?"

"I don't know. Your call, dude." I say while putting my book in my lap again and face it towards him. Hopefully he gets the hint that I don't want to talk.

"Well, I'm glad you're here, Lucy. I want to talk to you about something."

Guess he didn't get the point. I guess I need to step up and be there for him. Mom's not going to be back for a while. Chuck probably needs someone to listen. I mean, he's practically my dad. Well, the only one I've ever known anyway.

"What's up? How are you feeling?"

"I'm fine." He nudges the bags of take out. "I wanted to have a nice date night with your mom. But, that's obviously not going to happen."

"No, it's not. Sorry dude. Well, I'm going to go back to reading. Enjoy your dinner."

He nods his head and gets a bowl.

"Wait. Before you sit back down again, I wanted to know your thoughts on something."

If he says he wants me to start working again soon, I'm saying no. A part of me never wants to go through those doors again. The image of the blood on the floor and Raymond's bullet-filled head won't get out of my head. Aisle three is haunting my dreams. Or should I say nightmares?

I sigh, "Sure, what is it?"

As he pours the orange chicken over his greasy chow mein in a bowl, Chuck says, "This weekend, I think we should have a huge birthday celebration for me turning 40. You know how when it's someone's birthday they get the day off? I think we need to do more than that. Right?"

"Yeah, the day off is my favorite birthday present every year. What's your plan then? Am I in charge of all this? Please don't put me in charge."

"No, Lucy. You and your mom are going to be my assistants for the day. I was thinking some team building would be fun. Everyone, including their families, is invited. We can even buy a piñata. I know you love those!"

"Yeah, I liked piñatas when I was ten. I'm almost eighteen, remember?"

"I know you're almost 18. How could I forget? Anyway, I know you love birthdays. Not more than Christmas, though. I know you loved it when I dressed up as Santa Claus."

Last year, Chuck dressed up as Santa. He told me all week Santa was coming. I know what you're thinking. Most seventeen-year-olds don't get excited about Santa and you're not wrong. But I wanted to get in the holiday spirit. I was trying to break my grumpy attitude that happens on the holidays. When the twenty-fifth came around, he showed up at the house in the red suit and white beard. However, I don't think the real Santa has vodka and candy cane stains on his suit.

"Anyway, dude, let's hurry this up. I want to finish my book and chamomile tea," I say, trying to get the picture of Chuck as Santa out of my head.

"40th birthday party. You. me. Your mom. Sound good? I'm going to start planning when I finish dinner. I'm looking forward to this. Love you, Lucy. You're the best. Oh, wait, I have something for you!"

He digs through the bags and throws me a pack of powdered donuts.

Chuck surprises me with his kindness from time to time. A smile reaches my mouth. "Thanks, dude. I wanted some sugar." I give him a thumbs up and continue reading.

Powdered donuts stop my pity party for a few minutes. But then, I remember people coming over. The idea of having everyone at the house who works at the store is enough to give me an anxiety attack. I don't want to talk to anyone. Especially if it includes talking about Raymond.

But, I breathe through it and remind myself Chuck probably needs this. I also need to schedule a therapy appointment.

So, I guess it's actually happening. We're having a birthday party for Chuck. Everyone's supposed to be here in two hours. I'm already ready for them to go home.

Honest question here. When do people stop having themed parties? I want to say ten or eleven, right? Mom thought it would be a great idea to buy a bunch of tiki decorations for Chuck's party. We're having a luau. It feels racist and dumb, but she doesn't seem to care about either one of those. Also, he's turning forty, not seven. But I don't want to be the one who bursts her bubble; she's so excited and getting everything ready.

Ben and I are in the kitchen blowing up the balloons she bought at the dollar store in town. I told mom, "Wear the black wig from that witch costume a few years back." I feel like changing her hair color would fit in great with going all out for Chuck's birthday.

The smell of burned cake fills the kitchen. Red velvet is the only cake Mom makes for birthdays. Since he's the tallest out of us all Ben and I decided he'd hang up the piñata later, we stuffed it with lots of candy. We'll put it under the willow tree I named Fred when I first moved into Chuck's house. The snacks are done and the cooler's filled with drinks, though the ice is melting fast. With Chuck turning forty, my mom's hoping to have healthier snacks. Snacks he hates like carrots, celery, and pretzels. His doctor told him to stop eating so much red meat. He's even starting to take heart medication.

My mom corners me in the kitchen. "What do you think, Luce?"

"About what…?"

"My outfit, of course." She tosses her hair back and forth like a hair commercial.

Mom dyes her hair bleached blonde every week. I'm not talking about dirty blonde. Think more like white hair, as if she was walking through a snow blizzard. She spends about five dollars on a box and usually looks pretty good for the first few days before her roots start growing again. My mom's a natural redhead, so her hair gets a little ashy sometimes. Much to her frustration, the gray is starting to come through more and more now. She also spends about three hours a day putting on makeup.

"Mom, it's Chuck's 40th. I don't think people are going to care what *you're* wearing."

"You know I'm kidding, Lucy. I wanted to see what you thought. Can't I wear heels with pink Hawaiian flowers and get one compliment from you? Is that too much to ask?" She slams the back door leading to the garage, cigarettes, and neon-pink phone in hand.

Ben looks at me with his eyebrows raised. "What crawled up her ass?"

"I don't know. I'll go find out." I head for the smoke-filled, boiling garage. There're boxes filled to the brim with Christmas decorations, winter clothes, and we seem to be collecting spider webs like Halloween decorations. I rarely go in here. It gets way too hot for me.

She's scrolling through the selfies on her phone and her contoured face is lit up by the bright screen. "Mom, what's going on? Are you okay?"

"Yeah, hun. Everything's great."

"Cut the shit. You aren't on a talk show. It's me you're talking to." I notice her hair is parted on the left side. She never does that. Her eyeshadow's so heavily painted, she looks like a raccoon.

"I don't know anymore, Luce. Chuck hit me last night and gave me a black eye. He keeps saying it's going to stop, but it doesn't. I'm so lost."

Chuck hit her? A shiver goes down my spine. When I last saw him, he was so sad. Why would he hit her? I didn't know Chuck could get violent like that.

"Chuck hit you? When?"

"He hit me when I came back from the bars a few nights ago. He was upset that I'd been drinking without him."

"What? Are you serious? That doesn't sound like Chuck at all."

"Do you think your own mom would lie to you?"

"No. I'm totally surprised. What can I do?"

"Nothing. I'm getting us out of this shit hole, though. We can go to Seattle like you want. My treat, baby girl."

"Thanks, mom. Arizona sucks. I want to go now."

My mind feels like it's in a permanent crimson fog of Raymond. I know I need to get out of here. With or without mom.

She shrugs and lights another cigarette. "I know, monkey. We'll figure it out." I hear a truck pulling up to the house. Chuck must be home.

Breathe in. Breathe out. Let the fake and forced smiles begin.

My mom stands, squirts on her stripper smelling perfume that lives in the garage and flattens down her freshly made bleach-ridden hair.

Before her neon orange manicured hand reaches for the silver door-knob, she pops two pieces of watermelon bubblegum in her mouth.

I give her a thumbs-up as the door swings open. "You good?"

She winks. "Never better."

Oh, no. I know what that means. She's not great, and she's going to drink way more than usual. Ben knows this, too. Unfortunately for Ben, his mom says something similar. Except her substance of choice is Tennessee Whiskey.

He walks towards me and squeezes my hand. It all comes out in a rush, "Can we tell everyone to go home? We didn't even invite them. I don't want to be around people. Are you okay?"

"Ben, slow down. I don't want them over either, but everyone's probably already on their way. I'm fine."

Immediately, I realize I haven't lied to him in a long time. I don't like the way that feels with him, but anything is better than the anxiety plaguing my brain.

Can I hide away forever? Where's Chuck? This was his idea and still no sign of him. I send him a quick text, *'Where are you? Every-one's on their way.'*

I send a quick text to my therapist, too. *'Can we meet soon? I need to talk.'* I stuff my orange android into my pocket and inhale.

I find myself jumping from one mood to another.

I feel excited for cake. Now, I feel like I want to sleep and wake up in Seattle. I hate this. I remind myself of the mantra my therapist and I worked on during our last session.

My bipolar doesn't define me.

My bipolar doesn't define me.

An hour into the party and Chuck still isn't here. Rosa, her grand-daughter Nina, her son Julio, and their dog Alonzo are though. I'm not a fan of dogs, but Alonzo's super cute. He's a black Labrador and only weighs about twenty pounds if I could guess. Since he's still a puppy,

Alonzo's tripping over his paws. It reminds me of the first time I learned to roller skate.

Nina comes up to me and asks, "Lucy, can we hit the piñata now?"

"Let's wait a few more minutes until Chuck gets here. I also think more people are coming. Is that okay?"

She nods and goes back to petting Alonzo. I notice Mom's pouring herself another drink. I don't try to count her drinks since it's none of my business, but I'm pretty sure this is number five. "Mom, have you heard from Chuck? Nina wants to hit the piñata and a part of me wants to as well."

She adds a drop of lime sparkling water to her white tequila. "What was that, baby girl? How's my hair look?"

"Your hair looks fine. I asked if you've heard from Chuck. I don't know if you've noticed, but he's not here yet."

"Yes, I just heard from him. He's going to pick me up some cigarettes and then make his way home. I think he went to the bars or something."

"He better get here soon. People want to hit the piñata. You need to stop smoking, Mom. It's going to kill you one of these days."

"After this pack, I'm going to quit. Promise."

I roll my eyes and make my way back to Ben. He looks cute smiling with the puppy. I hope Snowball doesn't see him so happy. She might get jealous.

The doorbell rings. Why would Chuck ring the doorbell? Doesn't he have house keys? He can't be that out of it, right?

Ben answers. The dark-blue door swings open, revealing a swarm of people.

I say, "Hey, everyone. So good to see you outside of work!"

I immediately back away to ensure no one tramples over me. Everyone meaning, Michael and Joseph, the two main cashiers, and their wives, Leslie, and Grace. Leslie's hand covers her beach ball stomach, and she looks like she's about to pop any minute. I also see the two new hires with names I can't remember, one I think work in the frozen department and the other stocks the shelves.

A little girl with a teddy bear runs in as swift as a marathon runner. She doesn't look familiar at all. "Stella, come back here, sweetheart!" says Craig, the assistant produce manager. He waves at us as he tracks down Stella. She better not mess up any of our decorations.

I follow Craig into the kitchen since I want something to drink. Do I talk to him?

"Hey, kiddo. How are you doing? Happy graduation, by the way," Craig hands me a neon-pink envelope with my name in all capital letters and a heart.

"Thank you so much. I wasn't expecting anyone to bring presents."

"Lucy, you only graduate high school once. I know Ben and you want to escape to Seattle. This will help a little with gas on the way there."

"Thank you. I appreciate it. Do you think Stella would want to hit a piñata? I got one for the kids. But let's be honest, I want to hit it too."

Craig chuckles and fishes out a beer out of the cooler. "Stella, come on, sweetheart. Are you ready to hit the piñata and get some candy?"

Stella jumps up and down with Nina. In perfect harmony, the two girls say, "Candy! Candy!"

"Hey, Ben, I need your help. Sorry, Grace." I say.

"No worries, Lucy. Talk to you both later."

We race into the garage and obtain the sacred piñata. I didn't realize how heavy this thing was when we stuffed it earlier. I guess I got carried away with the dark chocolate and lollipops. Ben picks up the one old wooden baseball bat we still have. At one time, I wanted to join softball. Chuck was my coach and everything. I stopped going because I got nervous from everyone watching me at games.

"You guys look pretty excited about that piñata. Think I'll be able to hit it too?" my mom says while taking drags off her pink lipstick-stained cigarette.

"Of course, Mom. Is Chuck back?"

"No, not yet. Luckily, I had one cigarette left in my pack."

"Yeah, luckily. See you later." As Ben and I enter the house, I hear Chuck. Well, his laugh at least.

"And then I asked them, do you know who I am? I'm Chuck Williams, bitch. Then they gave me my meal for free. They must've seen my arms. I mean, they do look like pythons," Chuck tells Joseph while holding a beer in both hands.

I set the piñata down and put my hand on Chuck's shoulder. "Hey, dude, where have you been all day? We've been waiting for you."

"Lucy, Lucy! Calm down. I went to get a few drinks with my boys. No big deal. I can handle myself."

"Your boys? I have no idea who you're talking about. Anyway, Ben and I are setting up the piñata for the kids. You're welcome to join if you want." I open the door to the garage, take a rope for the piñata, and make my way outside to the hot Arizona sun.

Alonzo's sniffing everything in sight. The noise of everyone talking at once feels like a giant wave swallowing me whole. I'm feeling overwhelmed. I try to ground myself. Grounding means that you connect with your physical self and surroundings. It's a way to keep yourself present and not in your head. Another trick from my therapist. It usually works.

I see the adorable black puppy.

I see the red piñata.

I see the brown tree bark.

"Okay, Ben, let's get this party started," I say and hand him the brown rope.

After many swings to the head, the piñata is dead. His tiki brains are the only kind I'd eat and they taste delicious. Nina and Stella surprisingly had quite forceful swings and all the adults, including Ben and me, took a swig at it, too. I feel a sense of accomplishment combating it. Helping Nina and Stella was fun, too. They are super cute. I guess little kids aren't so bad.

As if we needed more sugar, Mom calls from the house. "Cake time, everyone!"

I don't want cake at all, especially red velvet. But Mom took a long time making it today and I should at least have a bite. As everyone piles into the kitchen, Mom and Chuck stand over the red velvet cake. Mom's hair is in three different directions and her makeup has smeared so much that her black eye is nearly visible. Chuck has an open bottle of vodka that's already halfway gone. This is all so incredibly embarrassing. I hate alcohol.

Mom takes the candles out of the drawer. "How many this year, Lucy?"

Ben shouts, "Forty, of course! You know this. Don't you?"

She laughs. "Oh, wow. I could forget that…"

Chuck takes a big drink and slaps Mom on the butt. "You forgot that I'm turning 40? Where is your brain, my love?"

Watching them interact makes me cringe. The way he looks at her feels like love. How could I be so wrong?

The candles light up the entire kitchen. Everyone has their phones out singing to him. People singing to you must be one of the most awkward things in the world. Chuck is handling it very well, though. His smile is as white as some piano keys. He looks very happy.

On the verse, "Happy birthday to Chuck…" he passes out. I don't mean the hand on the forehead stereotypical bullshit you see in movies. I'm talking full-on, vodka in hand, passing out. He didn't make any noise. Just fell over. My only hope as that he didn't crack his head open or anything.

Mom pulls out a new cigarette and lights it in front of everyone. "Lucy, check if he's okay."

CHAPTER THREE

I rush to his side to make sure he's still breathing. Fortunately, I see his chest moving. His heart must be beating.

I shake him. "Chuck, are you okay? Wake up. We haven't even had cake yet!"

Mom finally walks over after a few seconds. "Oh, my poor Chuck. Whatever will we do, Lucy?"

"What are you talking about? You didn't care less than a minute ago."

"Oh, baby girl. They don't need to know that. Shush."

Chuck sits up and starts drinking his vodka again. "Whoa, what happened?"

"Man, you passed out. Are you okay?" Michael asks.

"Yeah, man. I'm fine. None of my vodka spilled, perfect. Can we eat cake now?"

I feel so uncomfortable. My brain makes it so I'm back on aisle three. The red on the cake reminds me of Raymond's blood. I want to whisper to Ben, "I'm going to pass out like Chuck. I need to breathe."

But he's saying, "Yes, we can definitely eat cake."

By some miracle, I'm able to hand everyone a piece of the burned red velvet cake. I can tell not everyone likes it by the looks on their faces. But for Mom's sake, I think they're pretending to enjoy it.

Suddenly, my chest is tight and mid-bite, I run to the bathroom. I start crying. I try to push the tears away, but my body won't let that happen. I'm so tired of having two drunks as parents and I want to get away from dumb Arizona. I wish they didn't ruin everything with their drinking. Is that too much to ask?

While I feel like my eyes are running out of tears, someone knocks on the bathroom door. "Lucy, are you okay? You didn't finish your cake."

I open the door a crack and pull Ben inside. "Yeah, I'm fine. I'm depressed about my mom and Chuck. Will they ever stop drinking? I don't know how much more I can handle."

"It's hard, LL. I know. But there's nothing we can do about it. Have you taken your meds today?"

"Yeah, I took them. I'm beyond upset. My life fucking sucks."

"Umm, excuse me? Your life sucks? What about me? I mean, look at my mom. She's always drunk. It sucks that we both have shitty parents."

"Sorry. You definitely don't suck. I don't understand. Why am I not enough for them to stop drinking? I'm tired of being more of a parent to them than they are to me. When will this stop?"

"I honestly don't know, Lucy."

"I mean what does alcohol have that I don't? I'm actually alive and don't make them have hangovers. Can we leave for Seattle now?"

"No, we have a few more weeks left. You need to wipe your face and breathe, Lucy. It's not always going to feel like this."

"Life better not. I don't know how much more I can handle. I wish they'd love me more than alcohol."

"Oh, stop. You're much stronger than feeling sorry for yourself. You're going to be okay."

He's right. I need to stop feeling sorry for myself.

As I walk back into the kitchen, Chuck claps for me. "There's the daughter I never had. Glad you could join us."

"Thanks, dude. How's your head?"

He rubs it and then starts crying out of the blue. I haven't seen Chuck cry in a long time.

Between his tears, like a bolt of lightning, anger hits his bones, "I want all you good-for-nothing people out of my house right now! You've been here too long."

Everyone looks confused but shuffle out. Chuck's face is now so red, a stop sign would be jealous. His hands are grasped so tightly around the vodka bottle, his veins are popping through. I hope he stops drinking soon.

"You heard the man, out!" Mom says with a clear plastic fork in one hand that's been taken over by the cream cheese frosting. The other hand, she has a cigarette. Of course.

As the party flees like they saw a ghost, I follow them to the outside world. The hunched shoulders and sad faces lead me to believe no one wanted to go home this soon. I exchange a few sorry's and thank you's to everyone for coming, but the only one to respond is little Stella.

She gives me a hug and says, "Happy birthday. I love the chocolates, Lucy. Bye-bye."

"Bye, Stella." I'm pretty sure my heart melted. She's so precious.

As she leaves, I get sad again. So much for a fun party. Maybe I wasn't meant for a normal life like everyone else. I mean, having parents who don't drink and truly love each other is a fairy tale.

No one gets it all, right?

My eyes flicker with images of the past. With everyone gone, I'm trying to remember my childhood. My present life is way too sad to focus on.

Before Chuck, we lived in this tiny apartment across from my elementary school. I was only five and in kindergarten. The bone-white apartment walls were so thin, I could hear our neighbor, Mrs. Chang, brush her dentures every night. Mrs. Chang was the best neighbor ever. Her apartment always smelled like fried egg rolls and she always offered to babysit when Mom went to the bars on Saturday nights.

But the night that stands out the most is when she met Chuck. It started out like any other. I knew how to make peanut butter and grape jelly sandwiches by then, so Mrs. Chang didn't have to watch me.

Instead, she would knock on the nearly hollow walls to make sure I was okay. "Miss. Lucy, are you all right?"

"I'm fine. Are you?"

"Yep. Let me know if you need anything, sweetheart. I'll be here with the cats."

I'd go back to watching the movie, after I confirmed I was fine. I loved escaping into movies with wizards, elves, and magical worlds. The characters were enough company for me when Mom was gone. The different worlds helped me avoid how sad I was in this one. I always imagined the characters as my friends.

That night, Mom tried on at least ten different shades of lipstick, from grape purple to cherry red. She even put a bright pink lipstick on me.

While applying the lipstick, she said, "Here you go, baby girl. You can look like your momma who just turned 23! Stacy will be here soon. She's going to borrow a pair of shoes. What do you think of mine?"

I looked at her shoes in pure amazement. They were shiny like disco balls.

"Kelly, open the door. We gotta hurry!" Stacy shouted as her fist pounded the hollow wood.

I opened the door and she bent down to give me one of her famous hugs. Her hugs are so tight that I can barely breathe. Mom used to tell me she didn't like Stacy much. But she always brought over alcohol to drink before the bars, so she was important, I guess. That night she didn't need the ID, though. Stacy finally decided on some red-velvet heels and they were gone like the autumn-colored leaves in winter.

According to Chuck, their first conversation went a little like this:

"Hey, you're that girl with the kid, right?"

"Yeah? What's it to you? Do you have a problem with that?"

Before Chuck could formulate some kind of response, he told me Mom walked over to the jukebox. She requested her favorite Beatles song, *Lucy in the Sky with Diamonds,* which I'm named after.

Chuck walked up to Mom again, the bar lights creating a yellow glow on her hair. As he loves saying, 'Her white tube top showed off her newly pierced belly ring' that ring was a birthday present to herself a few days before. He says Mom's eyes looked like two perfect emeralds.

"Hey, you wanna dance?" he asked with a nervousness of a teenage boy at his first dance.

"Only if you buy me another drink."

Mom got her strawberry Cosmopolitan and they danced the night away. We moved in with Chuck a quick two weeks later.

The more I think about it, the more I realize that alcohol is such a huge part of their relationship. It's gross. I'm never going to drink.

Waking me up out of my trip down memory lane, my phone vibrates and I open my texts.

It's my therapist, *"Hey Lucy. When can you meet this week?"*

I close my phone and don't respond. I don't want to deal with anyone right now.

I hear a knock on my door. "Lucy, Lucy! Let me in." Mom. What does she want? Ben's passed out next to me. I hear his snoring.

I get up and open the door, "What do you want, mom? I'm going to take a nap."

"I was going to see if you could take me to the liquor store. I ran out of vodka."

"No, I'm not taking you anywhere. You need to stop drinking."

She puts her heel halfway through the door, so I can't close it on her. I hate this. Out of nowhere she says, "You're such a loser, Lucy."

"Umm...thanks?"

"You think you're all cool because you have a boyfriend and you're moving. Moving to Seattle. How original." she says while using her finger to pretend throwing up. I try to ground myself and notice the colors around me. But, it feels impossible. I feel my chest and arms tighten.

I can only take shallow breaths. "Mom, shut up. You're drunk. Got to bed." I say and slam my door in her face.

"Fuck you, Lucy!"

The slam must've been loud because Ben wakes up. I feel tears coming down on my face again.

Mom pounds the door again, "Lucy! Open up!"

Ben rubs his eyes and says, "What's going on?"

"Mom's trying to make me take her to the liquor store. She ran out of vodka."

"Should I take her? She's going to keep knocking."

"No! Don't open it. She called me a loser." I say while my throat goes completely dry. My cheeks are flushed. I feel as warm as a campfire.

Ben gets up and says through the door, "Lucy isn't feeling very well. Call one of your friends or something."

She says, "See, I told you! She is a loser. Can't even handle a little bit of sun." We hear her heels glide her away from my room. Thank God.

Ben glances at my desk that's strewn with orange and white pill bottles. "What ones do you take for anxiety?"

I can't think straight because of everything that's happened. I blink and see red blood. I see mom's glassy, drunk eyes calling me a loser. Is she right? Am I a loser? I mean, I'm still thinking about Raymond and it's been almost a week.

I try to remember what pills I take for anxiety. I haven't been taking my pills long enough to remember. "They're blue I think."

"Okay, these." he says while handing me a cup of two-day-old water and 2 teal pills. I swallow them quickly, so the bitter taste doesn't stay on my tongue. I put my head on my pillow and hold back even more tears. I hate my life.

I wake up in my clothes and look at my bedside clock, 3:15 AM. My room feels like a sauna. Ben passed out next to me, too. I take my pants off to prevent myself from spontaneously combusting.

I give Ben a huge hug and shut my eyes in hopes of a better day when I wake up.

Ben's lying next to me reading this book called *Alien Felines*. He seems to like it because every few minutes he laughs and the bed shakes. The book's what one would think—aliens turn into cats and attempt to take over Earth. I roll over to face him and say, "Dude! I passed out. What did you give me?"

"Well, good morning, sleepyhead. I gave you two of your blue pills. You said they were for your anxiety. I figured you needed all the help you could get."

I bounce out of bed like a pogo stick and look at the pill bottles. I notice that my emergency sleeping pills are open. They are blue, too. My psychiatrist prescribed me sleeping pills when I told him I have trouble sleeping. I haven't tried them yet, but he did tell me to only take half.

Shit.

"Dude, I'm only supposed to take half of one of these!"

Ben sets his book down and exhales, "How was I supposed to know that? They were sitting there and you said blue. Are you going to die?"

"No, I'm not going to die. I need to label things better."

"I'm so sorry, Lucy. It's all my fault. I hope you're not mad. Didn't mean to hurt you."

I give him a kiss on the cheek and say, "It's fine. Not mad at all. I slept well. It's okay. Just can't do it again."

I open up my regular pills and take them all in the right doses. I go back to the bed and feel a wave of tiredness hit me again. I look down at my phone and it says 11:37! Did I really sleep that long?

I hear my phone buzz again. It's a message request from Facebook.

I open it and the name reads, *Tiffany McBride*. Who the hell is that?

"Mom, come here!" I shout from my bed.

Mom pops into the room with a black mascara tube in her hand. Her left eye is the only one that looks like she's put it on. "Well, good morning to you, too, my love. How are you? Did you sleep well? Can I make you two some breakfast?"

She's usually super nice the next day after a binge. A part of me is still mad, but I usually forgive her. I mean she's my mom after all. The only one I'll ever have.

"No, I don't want any breakfast. But, does the name Tiffany McBride mean anything to you? She sent me a message on Facebook..."

She looks down at the ground and her mood seems to shift. Mom will sometimes go from super mean to putting on a show. A show like those ridiculous ladies on TV on infomercials who try to sell you a vacuum.

"That's what you had me come in for? Someone messaged you on Facebook? I need to get ready, Lucy. I'm supposed to be at lunch in ten minutes with Chuck."

She closes the door behind her and I'm so confused.

"What does the message say, Lucy?" Ben's peering over my shoulder.

"I don't know yet. I haven't opened it."

I open the message from Tiffany and read it aloud. *"Hello, Lucy. It's your aunt. Remember me? I know we haven't seen each other since you were born, but I thought I'd give this a shot. If you talk to your mom, tell her your grandpa, Frank, died yesterday. I'm living in Washington State, but have been in Arizona for the last few months to be with him. Can we meet up? Love you."*

Aunt? I have an aunt? Why did mom never tell me?

With learning I may have family and Raymond's murder, I'm going to lose my mind. More than I originally thought.

To distract me, Ben puts a movie on and makes us some macaroni and cheese. I haven't eaten yet. Cheese is also my favorite food.

I nearly put a bite of the white cheddar in my mouth and hear mom.

"I already told you a million times, Chuck. I'm going to the bars tonight. You can come with me or stay home. Your choice."

Guess their lunch got cut short.

"All I'm asking for is one time being put first. You're always going to the bars. What about me, Kelly? Don't I matter?"

"Are you an idiot? I always put you first. You need help, Chuck if you can't see that."

"My dad died, Kelly. More than ever, I need a family right now. Why can't you see that?"

"Stop feeling sorry for yourself. My dad kicked me out when I was 16. You don't see me crying over him! Get over it! He hated you anyway."

"Fuck you. I'm leaving. Don't call me."

I hear mom's heels come towards my door. I pray she doesn't come and try to talk to me. Too late. She knocks, "Lucy? Are you there?"

"Yeah. What's up?"

"I wanted to talk to you about the message you got. I haven't been honest with you."

I get up and open the door. She's holding a bottle of clear tequila. Surprise, surprise.

She grips the bowl of mac and cheese I left on my dresser. She takes a huge bite.

"Sorry if you heard Chuck. He got mad at me for something stupid. But, I wanted to ask you about that message you got. Will you read it to me?"

I read it to her. She takes four big swigs.

"Well, the old man finally kicked the bucket. Surprised it didn't happen sooner," she says and takes a huge burp.

"That's your only response? Geez. That's bad, even for you." I know that I should be more upset about her response. My life is feeling like one disaster after another at this point. Nothing can surprise me anymore. "Have I even met Tiffany?"

"After I gave birth to you. I think I asked her for some gas money or something. We got in a fight and I never talked to her again."

"So, you mean to tell me that you haven't talked to her for almost

18 years because of gas money? You never thought of contacting her or your dad? Didn't you miss them?"

"What else do you want me to say? Should I cry or something? He kicked me out, remember?"

"I don't know. I've never had anyone in my life die besides Raymond. And he doesn't count. He was crazy. He also wasn't a blood relative."

"Well, my dad was crazy, too. Anyway, invite her over, I guess. Let's see what she has to say."

"Sure, sounds interesting to me. I'd love to see my long-lost aunt. Is Chuck still here? Has he met her?"

"No, Chuck has never met her. He left to go see some friends or something. I don't care."

A part of me feels bad that Chuck doesn't have anyone to go when things get bad. I know he struggles with getting sober, so hopefully he doesn't get too drunk. I know he's getting more and more upset about his dad because he can't talk about it with anyone besides me. He better not black out or something tonight.

"So, can I give Tiffany the address? Is that okay with you?"

"Sure. Whatever, Lucy. Let's see how it goes."

I give Tiffany the address and she sends me a thumbs up. Guess that means she's on her way.

My hands shake. My heart's racing. I'm going to throw up all my mac and cheese. I get to meet *my* family. What if she hates me? What if she regrets coming here?

Can things in my life be normal for like one day? Is that too much to ask?

CHAPTER FOUR

Tiffany bought me a kiddie pool. I don't think she realizes I've grown since the last time she saw me 17 years ago. I should be grateful, I guess, since the heat is coming here. I think the weather reports said it's going to be one hundred twenty next week. With the heat, I decided that we should all go inside.

Tiffany is here to figure out funeral plans with mom. My grandpa died in his sleep a few nights ago and she doesn't know what to do for the funeral.

While sitting at the kitchen table, Tiffany says, "Well, he didn't die alone. I was at his bedside until he took his last breath."

"Honestly, I don't give a shit, Tiffany. He kicked me out when he found out I was pregnant and I never heard from him again."

"Problems aside, a father is still your father. Dad still loved you until the end. He talked about you all the time. But he began to forget me a few weeks ago and it broke my heart. He even forgot Maria."

"Who the fuck is Maria?"

"Maria was Dad's caregiver before he died. She cooked and cleaned his room in the care home. The two of them also played lots of Bingo at the senior center. She even picked him up every Tuesday to get ice cream together."

"Do you think I give a shit about Dad and his ice cream? Also, shut the hell up about Maria. Maria is nothing to me. So was dad."

"You should care about Maria. He was the only person dad had to take care of him. She's coming in a taxi from the hotel we're staying at. She wants to meet you and Lucy."

I haven't heard my mom swear this much since Chuck forgot to pay the water bill last month and we had no water for three days. It was the worst.

"What do you mean, you invited her over here? Did you not think to ask me?"

"Well, no. I thought you'd be okay with it."

"Do you ever stop and think… Oh, wait, no. I forgot. You're a dumbass and only care about yourself. I wish you'd never even showed up here."

"Look, Kelly, I'm sorry. I'm so sad about all that's going on, all I want right now is family. I thought you, me, Chuck, Lucy, and Maria could have a little bit of a service for dad today. We could talk and celebrate the life of our amazing father."

"Fuck you. Fuck you big time! Dad was never family to me and you know this. I have no fond memories, except for when he kicked me out and I was finally free of his stupid rules."

"Don't be like this, Kell Bell. He loved you. You know that."

"Stop playing this dumb pity party, game. You're not the only one who lost your dad recently. Chuck's dad died last week and Chuck's a mess. If you could stop pretending like we were one big happy family, that would be great. You're getting on my nerves."

"Oh, my god. That's terrible. I was reading the news and a guy was found dead in the grocery store. Can you believe it? Something's definitely in the air."

"You idiot! That was Chuck's dad, Raymond. Raymond was the owner of the grocery store and someone shot him."

Tiffany turns pale and says, "Someone shot him? Have they found the killer?"

I chime in, "No, they haven't found the killer yet. I was actually there the morning he was killed. He was lying there in a pool of his blood on aisle three."

Tiffany runs over and gives me a bear hug. "Are you serious, Lucy? Are you okay? I can't believe you went through that, sweetie. I know that if that happened to me that my mood would be so up and down. I mean, they already are because I'm bipolar…"

"Yeah, I've been feeling off this week. I stopped going to school, but should be going back on Monday. Wait, you're bipolar?"

"Yep. Have been my whole life. I've been consistently taking my meds for 5 years. Never felt better. I still get depressed, especially now with dad gone. I also get manic and think it's okay to buy shoes that match my underwear."

My mom clears her throat, "Well, as much as I love this bonding going on between the two of you, I want a margarita."

"Yes! Margaritas. Let's drink some and celebrate both dads. They would've wanted that."

"Fine. You buy the stuff to make dinner. But this is the last favor I'm doing for you."

"Okay, we're in agreement, then. I'll buy dinner and you make the margaritas. I should probably tell you that I stopped drinking a few years ago. I was beginning to develop a problem…"

"Good. More for me then!"

For a split second, mom and Tiffany smile at each other. Is this what family's like? Smiling and laughing? Tiffany's phone rings, "Hey babe. Where are you?" The doorbell rings. A woman is at the door who I don't recognize.

She puts her hand out, "Hi. I'm Maria, nice to meet you. You must be Lucy."

She's about four-feet-eleven-inches and is wearing a huge turquoise cross that takes up almost all her neck and the ruby on her ring finger hides the skin underneath it. That thing could feed an entire country in Africa. She has shoulder-length purple hair, a gap between two of her super white teeth, and the American flag tattooed on her left arm.

I shake her hand and say, "Uh, hi. Yep, I'm Lucy. This is my mom…"

Mom shakes her hand, too. "Kelly. Nice to meet you. Check out that ring on your finger! That's beautiful. Wait, why does it look so familiar…?"

Ben waves, "Hi! I'm Ben. Lucy's boyfriend."

"Hi Ben! It's so nice to meet you all. Dean had only the nicest things to say about you all. It's nice to put faces to all of your names."

Ben and I look at each other confused. Why would my grandpa talk about us? He never even met me.

"Let me get something straight with you, Maria. I don't allow any liars at my house. Okay?"

Maria blushes and looks down at her feet. "Okay. But, I wasn't lying. Dean talked about *you* all the time."

"Me? Why would he talk about me? He kicked me out at 16. He could give a rat's ass about me or even Lucy here…"

Tiffany chimes in, "Well, I have one more piece of news for you all. I promise this won't be as depressing. No one else is dead in the family. I know you're worried about that one, Kelly."

Mom rolls her eyes and takes another drink out of her tequila bottle.

"Well, out with it then. What is it?" Mom says.

"Maria and I are getting married in October! I proposed."

Maria shows off her beautiful ruby. Her smile is as bright as a Christmas tree.

Maria says, "I came here from the hotel because I wanted Tiffany to not put too many surprises on you all. But, I can't wait to be part of this family. I get to be an aunt and sister!"

Maria goes in to hug mom, but mom steps aside so Maria bumps into the air.

"Are you serious right now? First, I haven't seen you for 17 years and you tell me that dad's dead. Now, you're telling me that you're marrying his caregiver. You're so fucking selfish."

Why is mom acting so crazy?

"How am I selfish? I wanted you all to meet my fiancé while we talked about dad. Simple as that. Dad would've wanted us to be happy."

"For the last time, dad didn't care about me at all!" Now, where is my margarita, bitch?" Mom's eyes have lost all their color. Her body's swaying side to side.

"No more tequila, Kelly. You should pace yourself."

"Okay, Autism boy. Now, give me the bottle back. Go play with your dumb toys."

Mom's right. Ben does have Autism, but it's honestly cool. He remembers facts about everything and he's always honest. Ben is 6'3 and weighs 300 pounds. Ben should've played football based on how big his arms are. But, he reminds me of a walking teddy bear and is so sweet.

Ben puts the tequila bottle on top of the fridge, so mom can't find it.

"Nope. Not giving you the bottle back. For your information, I'm not dumb. Autism makes me see the world differently than you. It's better than being full of alcohol the whole time."

Out of the corner of my eye, I see mom's hand go up. Mom tends to slap people when she drinks. I'm not about to let Ben be her next victim.

I block her and change the subject at lightning speed. "So, I know people were talking about buying some dinner at the store. I'll write you all a list."

"What kind of toys do you collect, Ben?" Tiffany says while her eye contact stays on mom.

"I don't collect toys. Lucy and I collect Pez dispensers."

Mom sighs, "Oh, good for you. An 18-year-old collecting Pez dispensers. Do you want a medal or something?"

"Shut up, Kelly! Just let people enjoy things." Tiffany says.

A part of me wishes I could give her a high five. However, that would start World War Three here, so I'm not even risking it.

I take a piece of paper and I write ingredients for my black bean tacos. Everyone loves them.

I hand Tiffany the list and her eyes scan the page.

"There's no meat on here. Are you all vegetarian or something?" she asks.

Mom burps and says, "She has refused to eat meat since she was a little kid. People used to think I was starving her. We'd go to restaurants and she'd only get french fries."

I say, "Eating animals is gross and not necessary. Also, did you know that one pound of beef takes 441 gallons of water? At that rate, we won't have a planet anymore if people keep eating cows. I mean…"

Before continuing my rant on meat consumption, Maria says, "I had no idea it took that much water to make meat. I grew up in the Philippines and meat is with every meal. My dad was a farmer and we had to eat it. Or we'd go hungry."

"Hear that, Lucy? She would have to go hungry. Guess your mom isn't looking so bad now, huh?"

"I never said you were bad, mom. I don't know where you're getting that from."

"I know what you think, Lucy, Mom frowns. "Always the pity me. I saw you at Chuck's party rolling your eyes."

Tiffany says, "Oh, quit it, Kelly. You're being a bully."

"Don't get me started with you, Tiffany. You don't want to open that can of worms. Now, go get me some tequila. I'm out." she says while crossing her arms. She must still be upset at Ben for hiding it.

Mom is so mean. I bet in her mind, she probably thinks she can say anything because she's being *truthful*. Just keeping it *real*. Disregarding other people's feelings doesn't make you truthful or real if you ask me. I wish I could pull Tiffany aside and tell her to not buy any more alcohol. Hopefully, she's smart enough to ignore mom's request.

Tiffany says, "Well, Maria and I will be back in a little. Going to get," she reads my list again, "some black beans and zucchini. Looking forward to your cooking, Lucy."

"No problem. Hurry back, I'm hungry."

Mom says, "Hurry back, I'm thirsty."

Ben and I go to my room, so we don't have to deal with mom's drunken state. I'd prefer talking to a piece of cardboard. At least the cardboard can't say mean comments.

The sun's going down, but the weather is still in the 100's. Disgusting. I think it's safe to say my mom's pissed. Like extremely pissed. Before Mom got upset, I kept ignoring Tiffany's requests to go to the store with them. The two of them didn't understand how a grocery store could bring me such angst, so I finally just told them. Maria and Tiffany were letting me talk about the murder and how it's affecting me.

Mom doesn't joke around. "If you don't leave in the next two minutes, I'll call the cops! Get out of my fucking house!"

"Come on, Kell Bell. Can't we talk about this?" Tiffany asks.

"No, we can't this time. I thought you and Maria being here would be good for Lucy to have some family around. But you came in and ruined that by filling her head with lies about how much of a *hero* Dad was. I didn't expect to be bullied."

"Fine. We're go."

Mom doesn't joke around about the police either. She knows all the officers in town. I guess it pays when they all want to sleep with her and hate Chuck.

"Wait! Come back." I chase after them. "Wait, Mom. Stop it! I want to know more about my family!"

"Lucy, this has nothing to do with you. Go to your room. Now." Mom says while taking shots of her brown tequila.

Still, I run out of the house. My eyes hunt for the red convertible Tiffany drove here, but it's gone. I wish I could've said or done something to make them stay.

My hair sticks to my neck because of the stupid heat, I see Ben in the doorway.

He gives me a bear hug, "Let's go in your room. I don't want to be anywhere near your mom."

"Totally justified. She's extra terrible tonight."

We run into my room to avoid getting caught. I go over to my closet and try to find a comfy shirt to wear. I find a black one with red flowers. It's too small and sticks to my stomach. I dig through my dirty laundry and find one of Ben's 3x shirts. Perfect. "Is it okay if I wear this?" I ask him while holding up his gray shirt.

I crawl into the bed where Snowball is already sprawled out. I turn on my laptop and we decide to watch Comedy Queens for the sixth time. While the catchy theme song starts, my hands shake. I feel so frustrated and angry. Why does Mom have to be like this? Can't I have a normal day for once?

After we watch 2 episodes of Comedy Queens, I turn it off and decide to look up little-known facts about cats. Ben says, "Hey! What was that for?"

"Sorry! I must research cats. Maybe pictures of their paws and whiskers will distract me. Nothing's working to turn off my brain."

"Whatever you say. I'm going to organize my Pez dispensers."

"Did you know that black cats are good luck in England? Or that they have two hundred forty-four bones! Also, a president even had a cat named Socks in the White House! Can you imagine living in the White House? I'd never have to cook a meal again!"

"Lucy, breathe. Close your laptop."

I lay down while my heart pulses through my hands. I drink some water and take a Lorazepam. A minute later, the pill slows down my heart and I feel a sense of calmness. I think.

I can hear Mom pacing the floor and I smell her cigarette smoke creeping under my door. She tends to chain smoke when she's upset. I hear her heels clanking on the hardwood floor and her voice loud on the phone. She'd never need a microphone with a voice like that.

Her phone's on speaker while she talks to her best friend, Jane, in California. "He's such a dick, right? I hate him."

Ben and I ignore her. He's still organizing his dispensers. He's collected over fifty in the past three years, mostly from thrift stores. I'm always trying to find the most unique ones I can for him. Ben's favorite is a glow in the dark one with Jupiter on it. It's amazing that it still glows even though it's from the 1970s.

"Hey Luce, what's this?" He's holding a green envelope.

It has my name on it in a handwriting I don't recognize. The handwriting is slanted in a serial killer kind of font. It looks like the emerald-green envelope was stuck in someone's back pocket for a few weeks and is folded a few times.

My curiosity gets the best of me. I'm going to read it anyway. Couldn't hurt, right?

"I don't know. Throw it over."

I begin to read: *To my beautiful and unknown granddaughter. Hi, it's me. My name's Frank if you didn't know that. I'm dead now, which you hopefully have been told. But I'd like to give you some money for college, and the times I wasn't there. How's five thousand dollars sound? Good luck in this crazy, scary, but mostly beautiful world. May God be with you, or whoever you believe in. I've been an atheist my whole life, but whatever works for you.*

Dean

P.S. Don't always believe what your mom says.

"What is it? Is it a love letter?" Ben asks.

"Very funny. Not a love letter. Dude, guess what?"

"We're not playing this game again. You burned that bridge a long time ago when you told me that the drummer for Glitter Tooth was in the store last year."

"I've already told you this a thousand times, I'm sorry. The guy in the store was his twin!"

"Excuses, excuses. Out with it, LL."

"My dead grandpa left me five thousand dollars!"

"What? You're totally joking!"

I show him the letter and wave the check in his face. I'm in shock.

"Lucy and Ben, please get here right now!"

Shit, what does she need? Guess the plan to decide what to do with the money will have to wait until later. I swear that woman can smell any sense of anything good in this house and shuts it down right away.

"What is it, Mom?"

I wait for her response, but don't hear a word from her. I wonder where she went. I hear a knock on the front door. Better answer it, I guess.

I walk to the living room and look through the peephole. Mick Kane and some other police officers are here. I don't know what's going on. What are they doing here? Is Chuck in trouble? Did mom not pay her bar tab or something?

I try to find the trail of cigarette smoke that follows my mom around or the sound of her heels pacing the floor.

"Mom? Mom, where are you?"

Nothing. It's completely silent.

Wait, the toilet flushes in my mom and Chuck's room. So that's where I head. "Mom, the cops are here."

She jumps back when she sees me, "Lucy! Don't scare me like that. I didn't realize you were here."

"Well, I called a few times and didn't hear you. So, the cops are at the door. Did you call them when Tiffany was here?"

"No, I didn't call the police when Tiffany was here. Why are you always so mean to me? Just once, I'd like it if you treated me with respect, Lucy."

What's she talking about? When have I been mean to her? She needs to stop drinking.

We walk to the front of the house together and all I hear are the whispers and mumbling by Mick Kane and some other guy.

"Okay, Sullivan, let's make this quick. We need to find out what all the yelling was about. Someone should be home." says Mick Kane.

Mick Kane's one of those cops all the others wish they were. He's super quiet and intimidating at first, but he's nice once he warms up to you. He plays tuba on his days off at the bar, Dirty Sailor. His husband, Frank, is the human version of a cinnamon roll and they have two bull-dogs, Parker and Greta.

He keeps knocking on the door, faster by the minute. "Hello? Is there anyone there? Kelly? Lucy? I see your cars."

Before Mom puts her orange sprayed-on-tan hand on the silver doorknob, she grabs me in a bear hug so tight. It's almost as if our hearts are touching. I can't get a deep breath in and she smells of gummy worms, cigarettes, and tequila.

CHAPTER FIVE

"It was me, Luce… I killed Raymond. Don't forget me, baby girl. I'll get us out of this like I always do." She opens the door and walks out, letting all the humid air into the house.

She's lying. I know she's a little crazy, but she'd never kill someone.

"You killed Raymond?"

"I've been part of his dumb family and lies for way too long. Every time I saw him, I got more and more annoyed. The only logical way to get rid of him permanently. We're all going to be a lot happier now, baby girl."

I try to say something back, but I feel frozen in horror. I'm back on aisle three. His blood stains on the white floor. His shocked face. All because of her dumb mistake. My mom. A murderer. She's been carrying this around with no guilt.

I see a green wall. I see a dark-blue door. I see a package of neon-colored gummy worms.

Visualizing colors isn't helpful at all. My brain's still going in about fifty different directions. I can't focus on anything except my heartbeat pounding in my chest.

Ben walks into the living room while running his hands through his hair. "I'm thinking about this weekend... Shit, LL, are you okay? Where's your mom? What's going on?" He opens the white blinds on the front window beneath Chuck's sunken-in black leather couch with a confused look on his face. "Why are the pigs here?"

Ben hates the cops. He called them a few times when his mom used to beat up his dad and anyone she could—including Ben—after drinking. She's also spent all his dad's life savings on cocaine. His dad left his family a few days later because he was so heartbroken about everything. The cops knew all of this was going on, but had no grounds to arrest her or do anything about it.

My whole body shakes and my arms feel like I'm flexing. I want to fly away. I want to stop existing.

"My mom... is uh... the one."

Ben looks at me and stutters, "Uh...the one? What... are you... talking about?"

"Lucy," it's Mick again. Mick Kane. "Your mom's is in the police car. Want to say bye to her?"

Ben looks through the peephole and his entire body shivers.

He mouths to me, "What the fuck? Is this a joke? Do I open the door?"

I give him a thumbs-up, Ben does and Mick Kane comes into the messy dark house. The only things brightening the walls in here are the metallic letters on the old beer cans and the empty gummy worm packages.

"What's going on, Mick?"

"She's sitting in the police car and already spouting out orders. She requested some gummy worms for her first night behind bars. That mom of yours is something else, huh? Don't know how you deal with it."

Before I can respond, Ben says, "What's going on? What're you doing here? Where's Kelly? Lucy's not able to tell me."

"Well, listen here, son. Kelly admitted she's the one who killed Raymond. My boys found some interesting footage last night, and we barely had to question her. She told us all we needed to know. Never had a case solved so quickly."

"So, you're telling me, you fuckers never realized on the footage that it was Kelly? How dumb are you?" Ben's eyes turn black and his cheeks get rosy.

"Yeah, that's right. Slow down the language, though."

Ben relaxes a little and takes my hand. I look up at Mick with burning eyes and a choked-up throat. "I can at least say goodbye to her." I stand in the doorway with the police car in full view.

"Of course, kid. But make it quick. She's starting to get rowdy and violent. I don't want her hurting you too. You can come down to the precinct another day, and we can talk then. The station has pretty good coffee most of the time."

I look at him, gasping for air, and the right words. "How will I be able to talk to her? Can I send letters?"

"Yes, you can send letters. As I said, relax and try to get some rest. You can say bye to her now, since the next time you'll see her will probably be at her court date. I don't know how long until then, maybe two weeks. One more thing, though…" Mick says with a calm voice.

"Oh my God. What? What is it? What did I do wrong?"

"You did nothing, Lucy. We need to check around the house to make sure there's no evidence we may need. I don't know if there are guns or something that she's left around."

"Yeah, sure. Whatever." I go out the door while they come into the house.

Ben has his arms crossed in the doorway. He's watching them like a hawk and I'm glad he's here to make sure the cops stay in line. It looks like two new ones showed up out of nowhere.

I walk to the back of the stupid police car and open the door to give my mom one last hug. She's sitting there, her eyes puffy and bright red from crying. Her hands are behind her back in silver handcuffs.

I try to get her attention away from the handcuffs and the view in front of her. I wave my hand in front of her face, but she won't even flinch or blink.

"Mom, I love you. Don't forget me. I'll find a way to keep you safe."

A few seconds later, she says, "Don't worry, LL. I have a plan for this already. We'll go to Seattle. I promise. I'll call you as soon as I can, sis. Don't forget about me. God knows I'll be the best MILF in all of Arizona's jails!"

"Call me as soon as you can."

"Of course, baby girl. Will you please bring me…"

The cop that's keeping watch on mom, clears his throat. "Kelly. I don't want to have to tell you again. You aren't allowed to have anything with you. Just the clothes on your back."

"But, Bobby…" mom begs.

"That's it, we're out of here. Say bye to your kid…"

Mom spits towards his face and says, "Fine. I'll say bye, but my lawyer is going to have something to say about your treatment of me. This is harassment."

She has a lawyer? Since when?

"Bye mom. I love you! Call me when you can."

"Of course, baby girl. You're going to help me find a lawyer. You're so smart. I raised you right."

So, I guess she doesn't have a lawyer. The police car drives off and I wave until the car reaches the end of the street.

I guess she's actually gone. The sirens that were once so loud have turned into a faint silence of longing in my heart. I go into the house while my oversized black T-shirt is damp and sticky. My whole body tingles as I look at Mick, who's standing in the living room. "Did everything check out or whatever?"

Mick shouts, "Hey, Jones and Wolf, get over here!"

The first of the duo walks out of Chuck's room and puts her hand out. Her black hair is parted in the middle and pulled back into a ponytail. Her dark-blue eyes match her uniform. She has freckles all over her face, including her lips. "Hello, Lucy. I'm officer Jones, but you can call me Mallory."

I shake her hand. "Hi. Nice to meet you. Did you find anything?"

"Everything's clear."

Mick yells, "Wolf, get over here!"

The second officer, Wolf, towers over me. He has to be over six-feet-tall, is bald, and has bugged-out green eyes. He looks like an iguana. No joke. "Yes, sir. What is it?"

"Did you find anything that can be used as evidence? You know, the reason we're here?"

"Oh, yeah. Sorry. Uh, no. No, I didn't find anything."

Mallory rolls her eyes. "Oh, rookie, you have a lot to learn. We're heading back to the station."

Mick takes out his little white notepad and writes down his phone number. He also hands me his business card. It's white and black in a boring font. It's definitely the worst business card I've ever seen.

He says, "Please, call me whenever you need to talk to someone or if there's another emergency. It's going to be close to impossible, but try to process this all. Call a friend or a medical professional and discuss how your body and mind are feeling. She's in good hands. My best men and women are on top of things. She has screwed herself over, though. I hope you know that. Most people don't admit to killing someone."

I give him my number before I forget. I want to stay in the loop with everything that's going to happen. However, Mick's completely insane if he thinks I can relax with all this going on. My heart hurts. My bones ache. My legs feel like chocolate pudding on stilts. I feel like something knocked the wind out of me. My eyes feel heavy and are flickering like Christmas lights. I bet they have lost all their color.

I shut the front door and turn to look around the dark house. Ben and I are all alone. I always wanted this, but I didn't think it'd hurt this bad. Does this mean I'm an orphan now?

I guess she's actually gone. The sirens, once so loud have turned into a faint silence of longing in my heart. The blood-red and neon-blue lights, once overwhelmingly bright have now faded into the dull black of night. I don't know what to do. But I know all I want is to sleep for a week. And have everything back to normal.

I creep down the hallway, there is a knock at the door. It's a soft knock, so it couldn't be one of the steroid-filled cops or Mick Kane. It sounded like someone was knocking with hands made of cotton candy.

Two voices merge to become a high-pitched one. "Lucy, open the door! We miss you!"

My two best friends. Fuck. Sarah and Lauren are here.

I whisper to Ben, making sure they don't hear me, "Please, tell them I'm not here."

He's not the best at hearing quiet noises. "What? I can barely hear you. I told you, Lucy, you need to speak up."

Shit. My cover's blown. I creak the door open and slither out of the house like a snake. "Hi, girls. What's going on? Can I help you with anything?"

The girls, my best friends Sarah and Lauren, are here because I think we made plans to hang out. I have this problem where I always feel lonely and want people around, but the moment I'm hanging out with them, I want to go home. But now, I'm at home so I don't have to make up some lame excuse why I don't want to hang out anymore.

"Hey... What's going on? Were we supposed to hang out? Did I forget again?"

Sarah, the funniest person I know, is going to make some kind of sarcastic comment. I know it. She's not too hard to figure out.

She looks at me with her kind forest-green eyes and says, "Lucy, are you okay? We've been texting you the last two days reminding you that we had plans. We went to the store and there was caution tape all around the doors."

Wait, do they not know? In this small town? Where news travels faster than lightning?

I push them through the dark-blue door. I don't want any neighbors overhearing and spreading news like wildfire. Some of them are outside talking among themselves. Ben is lying on the couch, flipping through our over five hundred channel TV, trying to find something.

He'll probably end up watching a serial killer documentary. The girls have brown paper bags in their arms. I wonder what's in there.

Lauren, the more serious one, always wears a face full of makeup. Her hair is a different color every week. This week it's red like your upper lip gets when you drink too much tropical punch. She looks at me. "Lucy, what's going on? Are you sick or something? You seemed fine when we talked to you last…"

I gulp. "Nothing's going on. I'm fine. I feel a little weird, but I'm okay."

"You know you can always tell us what's going on, Lucy. Best friends don't keep secrets," Sarah says.

"Well, it's not like I've been avoiding you on purpose…"

"Okay, you're starting to scare me. You're not pregnant or something, right?" Sarah says while shooting eye daggers at Ben.

I laugh because the idea of me being pregnant is pretty crazy. "No, I'm not pregnant. There was a murder at Smiles and…"

Before I can finish Lauren says, "Yeah, we know about the murder. It's been in the papers and all over social media! Why do you think we showed up? You haven't responded to our texts for days. We wanted to make sure you're not fully in panic mode."

I am in full panic mode. I don't know how to convey that without sounding like I'm whining. I never want to be a downer. However, I try to remember that these are my best friends. Like Sarah said, best friends don't keep secrets.

I look down at the floor. Eye contact is hard for me when I feel vulnerable like this. "Well, to be honest, I am in full panic mode. I saw Raymond's dead body and was there the day after he was killed. I can't stop thinking about his shocked face and everything."

The two of them gasp in unison and immediately rush in for a bear hug. I usually hate hugs, but this feels comforting. I have great friends even if I don't always know how to be a good friend and not hide away.

After about fifteen seconds, I let go because the walls begin closing in on me again. I pull away and mumble, "Sorry, I can't handle too much touching right now. Ever since this started, my body is in full run-away mode. Seattle can't come soon enough."

Lauren tells me, "I wish I could say I understand, but I don't. I can only imagine what seeing a dead body would do to someone. Has your mom been there for you at least? I mean I know she's not the best at comforting, but she is funny sometimes."

Sarah nods, "Yeah, Lauren's right. I know growing up with a mom like her wasn't always the easiest, but she still cares in her own way."

I walk towards the fridge to pretend I'm getting something to drink, but end up falling to the ground in tears.

"My mom..." it's a stumbling of words, "she...did it."

Ben runs toward me and picks me up off the ground. He carries my limp body and puts me on the couch. Lauren and Sarah follow.

Sarah says, "Lucy, what? I can barely understand you."

I dig around my brain for the words to come out, but nothing. It feels like a nightmare I used to have when this creature chased me. He'd finally find me and I was never able to scream. My head tingles. My teeth start chattering.

Ben says, "Kelly killed Raymond. She's the murderer. They— the police took her away."

"WHAT?" Sarah yells, "Are you serious? When did all this happen?"

My brain and mouth are finally working together. "Literally less than 5 minutes before you got here. I had no idea she did it."

Am I an idiot for not knowing? I mean she has been acting angrier than usual.

Lauren says, "I'm honestly speechless, Lucy. What would make her think murdering someone is okay? Don't get me wrong, Raymond was pretty creepy, but this is next level."

Sarah scoffs. "Why are you asking her? It's not like she knows. Murdering people isn't genetic or something, Lauren."

Ben laughs, "Can you imagine if it was genetic, though? Your double helix having little guns etched into the polynucleotides!"

I giggle because the idea of little weapons on my DNA is pretty cute. Leave it to Ben to have me stop thinking for a split second.

Sarah asks, "Well, what do you need from us? As your best friends, we know that you hide away and don't answer your phone a lot of the time. But, this doesn't feel like the right time to hide away."

"I honestly don't know. Let's go sit and see if we can think of anything. I wish this all could go away."

We sit at the wood table in the dining room. There are silver beer cans all over, cereal bowls full of stale Tasty O's, Mom's half-eaten gummy worm packets, and a few unopened bottles of red wine Maria left here.

This house is gross.

I need to get out of here.

I find myself spiraling out of control again. I start biting my nails. My emotions want to take over and swallow me whole. I try remembering things my therapist taught me when I feel like this.

I remember our first session. She taught me something called grounding and ways to make myself more present. She said to recognize colors in my surroundings and by doing so, I become less in my head and more in the moment.

I'll try the color activity again. Maybe it'll help me feel like I'm here in the room and not on aisle three. I can't stop thinking about where Mom is and if she's safe. Here goes nothing.

I see blood on the white floor at Smiles.

I see Lauren's red hair.

I see Ben's yellow shirt. He looks like a human in a banana costume.

I feel a little calmed down. I guess I'll keep trying this color thing out. Sarah gets up from her chair and gives me a huge hug. She smells like oranges and cigarettes. "I'm going to ask you again. What can we do, Luce?"

"I'm not sure. Distract me. Take me on walks? I don't know. I can't take deep breaths. My head won't stop. This all sucks so much."

Sarah gets the biggest smile on her face. She looks like someone gave her a kitten. "Funny thing is, I brought distractions. Are you okay with that? I want to make sure I'm being a good friend."

"Honestly, anything sounds better than thinking of aisle three right now."

The room goes silent. I hear car horns in the distance and the neighbor's Ranchero music.

Lauren says, "Well, Sarah and I brought some things that may help you feel better…"

They empty the big paper shopping bags. There's a shit-ton of makeup in them. It looks like they robbed a makeup counter at the mall. There are blue, green, purple, brown, and silver glitter eyeshadows. Blushes in every shade of red and pink. Three packs of fake eyelashes. And for some reason, there's even some with blue on the tips of them. Strange world. I even see five tubes of mascara, which I've always feared. I think they make your eyelashes look like bugs.

Sarah says, "Lucy, do you know what day it is?"

"It's Saturday, right?"

"Yes. I'm glad you're not so far gone that you've forgotten. Well, with it being the weekend, you know what that means, right…?"

CHAPTER SIX

At this point, she and Lauren are on the edge of their seats. The moment the makeup hit the table, Ben went and sat down on the couch again. I'd rather be sleeping right now, to be honest. Or eating donuts. A chocolate donut with sprinkles sounds like perfection.

Lauren, who's been texting off and on since she's been here, blushes every time she puts down her phone. She sits next to me in my chair, so we're squished together. "Lucy, next Saturday's going to be the best day of your life."

I think they're on drugs. I want to look at them, but I don't want them to see how black my eyes are right now. I feel drained of all energy and strength. It hurts to even blink. "The best day of my life? What've you planned? You know I hate surprises."

Lauren's out of breath from all the excitement. She and Sarah are in total unison again and scream, "Prom night! It's a week away!"

Oh, shit. They're right. Before I can respond, my phone buzzes. It's Tiffany.

She texted me, "Call me, right now!"

Saved by the phone. Thank God. I look at them. "Guys, I gotta call my aunt. It's an emergency. I don't know if she knows about my mom yet."

Sarah looks through the makeup. "It's fine, Lucy. Do what you need to do. We'll be here. We aren't going anywhere."

Lauren leaps out of the chair and goes to the bathroom or something. I hear her giggling through the walls. My phone is like a floppy fish since my hands are so sweaty. I click on Tiffany's name. I hate talking on the phone, but I need to push myself.

There is no noise on the other end. I almost hang up, but then I hear a muffled voice. "Lucy, it's me! It's Tiffany."

"Hi, Auntie. How are you?"

Tiffany's voice comes in clearer now, but it sounds like she is crying or is underwater. "I'm okay. Just got off the phone with your mom. She was at the police station. Do you know what's going on?"

She called Tiffany and not me? How does she know her phone number? Why would she call someone she kicked out of her house? Well, nothing I can do about it now, I guess. I search for the right words. I don't want to come off as rude or bothered, even though I am.

"Yes. Ben and I were here when it happened. Pretty weird, huh?"

She sounds annoyed and distracted. I think she's talking to Maria. "Yes, I'm talking to Lucy. Yes, I'll tell her you love her. Sorry, Lucy. Maria says she loves you and I love you too. Where are you at, honey? We're still at the Mariachi. Does Chuck know?"

Shit. I totally forgot about Chuck. Well, not forgot, avoiding. I didn't want to be the one to tell him. Guess it's time to be an adult about all this. Maybe I can get Ben to do it.

"I'm at home. Ben's here and so are my best friends, Lauren and Sarah. We're planning for prom, I guess… Hello? Are you there?" It sounds like I'm echoing.

I hear Maria's voice. She sounds as excited as someone who just won the lottery or something. "Prom? Lucy, you're going to go?"

"Yeah, I guess. I don't want to, but I don't have a choice."

"Oh, darling, you must go. In the Philippines, as a little girl, I used to dream about school dances. We'll head over soon to talk about your dress, hair, makeup, everything!"

Tiffany gets on the phone again. "Sorry. My girlfriend gets a little too excited about the idea of dressing up and putting on makeup. Shit. I mean fiancé. Don't tell her I called her that! She'll kill me. We'll be there soon. Stay safe, Lucy."

"Okay, bye." Ugh. Why does this dance nonsense matter so much? I need to find Ben. He'll agree with me. Hopefully.

I hear him in the kitchen. "You guys know Lucy doesn't like or wear makeup, right?"

Lauren's getting all sarcastic, "Well, prom's definitely more important than sitting home or bidding on some guy's limited-edition Pez in Ohio or something. Besides any distraction from the murder is what Lucy needs right now."

Ben turns as red as his hair. His chest gets noticeably tighter. Please, please, don't say anything stupid. Before they can say anything else or start fighting, I come into the kitchen. It's silent and everyone's looking at me.

Ben looks concerned. "Luce, how was Tiffany? Does she know yet?"

Lauren and Sarah look concerned, too. "Did we do something wrong?" Why would they think they did something wrong? They've been everything I needed today.

"No, of course not. I'm so glad you're both here. My aunt and her fiancé are on their way over. Having you both here is helping, but I am still super sad." I burst into tears.

Ben squeezes my hand, "You have all of us, Lucy. We love you unconditionally."

"I'm an orphan now. I wish I had a grandma to make me chocolate chip cookies and say I'll be okay. What should I do? Where can I go?"

Sarah's crying, too. That girl could write greeting cards. "Well, Seattle isn't going anywhere, and you'll always have a family—Ben, Lauren, and me. No matter where we are. I mean, it's our last year of high school. We're all probably getting out of this stupid desert somehow."

Lauren's crying as well. "Yeah, Luce. I haven't told anyone yet and didn't want to hog the conversation, but I got a full scholarship for Alabama State to play lacrosse next year. Even with me being in the middle of nowhere in Alabama with all the cowboys and barbecue restaurants, I'll still be a video call away. And we'll always reunite for the holidays."

Sarah says, "Eww, does that mean we have to go visit you in Alabama? I thought Arizona was bad."

Lauren glares at her, "Wow, that was rude. Ignoring that. But, Lucy, murder sucks. Especially ones by your mom. Feel free to talk about it all you want, okay?"

Snowball's circling my legs and keeps meowing at me. She's always so empathetic and always knows when I'm upset.

Ben looks more relaxed now and gives me a huge kiss on the cheek. "You know I'm not going anywhere. You're stuck with me now, McBride, whether you like it or not."

I'm smiling from ear to ear. "Girls, you're making me almost barf from the cuteness. Thank you. I feel better now. But I'm starving. I think my stomach is eating itself. I want pancakes or donuts. I want to go out to eat for an all-carb meal."

Lauren, the most health-conscious out of us, winks at me. "Well, Luce, it's almost eleven. We can go to Holy Cow. They have everything. Pancakes for you and a salad for me."

Sarah enthusiastically says, "Yes! Holy Cow sounds perfect. Fruit and eggs sound amazing."

Ben shrugs his shoulders. He's usually up for anything. He looks at me. "I need more guy friends. This all-girl nonsense is going to drive me even more crazy."

Someone knocks at the door. Fuck. I wonder who it could be. I don't want to deal with any more people. I can barely handle myself right now.

Sarah says, "Do you want me to open it?"

Before I can answer, I run into my bedroom before anyone catches me and wants to talk. I realize now I haven't taken my meds yet either. My room's a mess. I see my time traveling book open to chapter six, my Cats by Candlelight records that were a Christmas present from Chuck last year, and my half-eaten dark chocolate with almonds bar is in clear sight. I seek out my orange-and-white-topped pill bottles to take my daily amount. I find them. I open the child-proof lids with some difficulty and annoyance that they put these lids on for adults.

I put two anti-anxiety pills and one mood stabilizer in the palm of my hand and chug the lukewarm water sitting on my nightstand. They always leave such a gross aftertaste in my mouth, which is why the chocolate bar sits so close to them. If I could describe the taste, all I can think of is pill-y and chalky. I don't feel better yet, but the panic becomes less tsunami-like. I hate taking pills and that I need them, but it's better than feeling such highs and lows all the time with this dumb disease.

My bipolar doesn't define me.

My bipolar doesn't define me.

I hear the voices of two women that aren't Lauren or Sarah. It's Tiffany and Maria. Thank goodness it's not a cop or one of my mom's stupid friends. They're always so nosy and want to know what I've been up to.

Tiffany's talking to Ben. "Here, bud, I got you something at the gas station in town."

Ben sounds excited. "Thank you so much! I'll have to show Lucy. Let me go find her, so we can all get some food. It's been a pretty emotional day."

I hear Ben turn the corner with his stomping feet and he sees me sitting on my constantly unmade bed with the purple pillows. "Luce, look what Tiffany gave me!" He's holding a Pez dispenser of some random cartoon character I don't recognize on it and puts it in the collection.

"Dude, that's so cool! Now, we whatever that is!"

The Pez dispenser is a cross between a cat and a lamb. It's neon purple and is pretty cute even if I don't know what it is.

Ben looks at the wrapper it came in and it says Dr. Spectacular. No bells are ringing. But, it's pretty cute.

He adds it to the other cartoon characters, "What do you think? It fits perfectly."

"Perfect." The Pez collection is super distracting and wonderful.

I'm so glad we have it. I know Ben never wants to put the candy in them, but a part of me does.

Tiffany knocks on the door, even though it's open. "Lucy, can I come in? Are you decent?"

Ben puts his hand in mine and squeezes tight. I take my neon-orange running shoes, some white socks, and put some deodorant on. I don't feel like smelling like sweat and sadness anymore. Fake flowers and vanilla are preferred. I can't seem to find a shirt that's not covered in Snowball's fur.

"Come in. I'm just getting my shoes on so we can get some food."

Tiffany sits on the bed to the left of me. It's like a Lucy sandwich now. Her wallet's fallen from her pocket. I feel boxed-in, but try not to show it. The last thing I want to do is seem annoyed at people who are doing the best they can to help.

She gives me a hug. "Your mom loves you, LL. She told me that her biggest concern in all this is your safety. She wants you to go back to school and try to live a normal life while she works on coming home."

A normal life? What does that even mean? Life wasn't even normal when she was here. "Thanks, Tiffany. I appreciate that. I'll try my best to stay normal."

Ben laughs, "You don't know how to be normal, Lucy. Don't force it too much."

"Lucy, whatever you need, I'm here. Okay? We're family and we'll figure this out. Together. I know your mom has her faults. She can be incredibly selfish and quite an angry drunk. Yet, she still is family." Tiffany says.

My life has gone from the shock of mom being a murderer to now people pouring their hearts out to me. I feel like one of those dumb family movies where they all wear matching Christmas sweaters and sing songs on a piano in perfect harmony.

I can't take it anymore.

I interrupt, "Listen, Tiffany. I appreciate you being there with all of this, but I should eat something. My doctor said if I take my meds before food, I can become prone to the side effects. Today's been enough emotionally. I don't want to add delusion or notice things that aren't there to the mix."

"Okay, I completely understand. Now that you mention food, I could go for some pancakes."

"I know just the place!"

"Lead the way!"

She gets up right away, puts her black leather wallet in her back pocket, and walks to the front door.

"At the dealership, I decided on a convertible since Maria somehow has never been in one. And now it's time for you to show me the best pancakes in Arizona."

Maria, Lauren, and Sarah get up from the makeup-filled table that is now filled with hair products and curling irons too. We all herd outside like chickens.

Where's Chuck? Should I call him?

I pull out my phone and text him, *"I'm heading to the Holy Cow with some friends. If you'd like to come, you're more than welcome."*

I stuff my phone back in my pocket that has messages from Lauren, Sarah, my therapist, and some girl that sits in front of me in Spanish class. I take some deep breaths.

I see Sarah's red hair.

I see Maria's big, white smile.

I see Snowball's white fur.

Lauren and Sarah ride to the Holy Cow, in Lauren's blue Corolla. She's named it Lola, it has sea turtle seat covers. The car's named after her good friend in England. She got her license a few weeks ago and she's been practicing her parking. She's getting good at it and even sends pictures of her excellent parking all over town.

Ben and I ride with Maria and Tiffany. I've never ridden in a convertible either. We roll down the windows and put down the top. The cool wind in my hair sounds amazing. The black sky is almost a deep purple, and the stars wink down on us. It almost feels like the stars are showing me that there's more to the world than just Arizona. There are galaxies. Planets yet to discover.

I see a shooting star and wish that all this will go away.

Ben's voice wakes me from my funk. "Lucy! Lucy! Anyone home?"

Startled, I see that we're at the restaurant. "Yes, I'm here. Sorry, I was thinking about Mom."

"I know. You'll probably think about her a lot for a while."

"You're right. But why did this have to happen? I'm so fed up with my mom being selfish all the time. She's supposed to take care of me. Not the other way around."

"Why can't we move to Seattle now? I don't understand. Is there something I don't know?"

My stern frown turns into a tiny grin. "No, we're still 100% going. I just wanted her there with us. Chuck's been such an asshole to her lately. I mean, you saw her eye, right?"

"Yes, but that doesn't matter right now. Golden brown pancakes and maple syrup do."

"Lucy, Ben, get over here! They're gonna eat without us." Maria says.

"Let's go, LL," Tiffany says as she puts out her cigarette and chases after Maria.

Ben grabs my hand and drags me into the Holy Cow. The Holy Cow is open 24/7 and always smells like grease and week-old coffee. Lauren and Sarah are already in the dark blue leather booth, waiting. They look so precious exploring their faded menus. The restaurant's full of old cowboys with their faded hats and leather boots and sad women who are alone looking at empty coffee cups. I hope they're okay.

"Lucy, you're doing it again! What are you going to get?" Maria asks.

I anxiously flip through the menu. Everything sounds so good. "I don't know yet. What are you all going to get?"

Lauren responds right away, "A side salad of course and some orange juice."

Sarah follows soon after. "Some fresh fruit probably and two scrambled eggs."

Ben looks as nervous as I am. He doesn't like being put on the spot. Especially being so outnumbered. "Uh, I've been craving bacon. I'm thinking French toast or the breakfast burrito."

Ben isn't vegetarian like I am. It used to cause a lot of fights since I was always trying to convince him to change to no meat, but I've learned to get over it because it's his life. Also, bacon smells delicious and I'm not ashamed to admit that. There are days I crave meat, too.

Our waitress, Patty, comes to the table. Her name tag is crooked, and so is her smile. She has white hair and looks like she could be my grandma. Her hands are full of wrinkles and look almost blue. I'm almost nervous to order from her because I don't want the plates of food to be too heavy for her old lady hands.

"How about a round of water for y'all?" right away, I notice her cute Texan accent.

Ben says, "Sounds great. Can I also get a root beer?"

Patty insists on taking more drink orders. "Anyone else want a drink besides the fella?"

"Make that two root beers, please," I say.

"Alright then. I'll get those two root beers for y'all."

I look back at the menu. Pancakes sound good. Should I add blueberries, strawberries, or whipped cream? French toast sounds good, too. I love cinnamon. Should I get grilled cheese? I like American cheese. It may look like plastic and is probably super bad for you, but it's tasty. It always reminds me of my childhood.

Patty's back. She seems to be taking it easy. She slowly puts the waters and root beers for Ben and me on the table. It's settling my anxiety knowing she's being extra careful. Everyone quickly gulps their water. We're all dehydrated from crying and it's still close to one hundred ten degrees out because we're in the stupid desert.

In her adorable old lady voice, Patty walks up to the booth and says, "Everyone ready to go?"

Everyone seems pretty sure of themselves. Fuck. Can't spiral again. Visual exercise begins!

I see a red ketchup bottle.

I see white creamer pods.

I see purple on the grape jelly packets.

I see silver forks on the green napkins.

Cute Grandma Patty looks at me directly. "What will you have, little lady? Everyone else ordered. You're up, sugar."

Without hesitation, I scream, "Strawberry waffles with extra whipped cream and grilled cheese with mashed potatoes!"

"You got it, sweetie. I'll put that order in right now."

I've never felt like this before. This makes algebra and biology feel like nothing. My heart almost feels like it's being squeezed because I miss my mom so much. I keep expecting a call at any minute from her needing a ride home from the bar, but deep down I know that won't happen.

I look at my reflection in my phone's screen and see my eyes for the first time since the cops were at the house earlier. Before I can look more and fix my messy hair, my phone vibrates.

It's Chuck. Do I answer?

Ben notices phone and takes my phone. "Lucy, your phone's driving me insane. It won't stop ringing. Call back whoever's making me jump every time it vibrates." He puts it in his yellow pocket. Almost all his shirts have pockets. I'm about to throw it out the window," Ben yells.

I know he's trying to protect me, but I still worry about Chuck. My attention is distracted and I want to help him feel better. He's the only parent I have left.

It's safe to say Chuck may be missing mom or he just got home and no one was there. Well, Snowball is, but he hates her since he's highly allergic to cats. He called me thirty times and texted me twenty-seven times.

"Lucy, where's your mom?

Is she in her class?

Where did she go?

Where are you?

Hello?

Are you getting my messages?

Why's the table full of makeup and hair stuff?

Lucy, please pick up the fucking phone! I need to talk to you or your mom right now!"

I call him back and it goes straight to voicemail.

I give him one more chance and he picks up on the first ring. "Lucy! You're alive. Thank God!"

"Of course, I'm alive, weirdo. Where were you?"

"I went to the bars, hoping your mom would show up, so we can talk through everything. She never showed. Is she with you?"

I want to tell him that mom's the murderer, but a phone call doesn't feel like the right way to tell him.

"No, she's not with me. I'm getting some food with my friends, Ben, Maria, and Tiffany. Do you want to come? We're just at Holy Cow."

"No, I've been drinking way too much tonight. I'll be here when you get back. Love you."

"Love you, too. Text me if you want me to bring you anything back."

I feel bad for not telling him, but this truth needs to be told face to face.

Tiffany winks at me. "Welcome back, stranger. Who was on the phone?"

CHAPTER SEVEN

Funny that she calls me stranger because we truly are kind of like strangers. But she's still a pretty awesome person, and she's the closest blood family I have at the moment. Well, come to think of it. She's all the family I have now. Fuck. This sucks.

"Just Chuck. He's looking for me and my mom. I feel bad because I want to be there for him, however my stomach is rumbling."

"Well, he knows you're alive at least. Not much more we can do for him right now." Ben says and shrugs.

Tiffany says, "Let's just eat and enjoy what's left of tonight. He can wait."

I don't want to talk to anyone about my mom, Chuck, or my feelings. I want my feelings to be in the form of a waffle covered in whipped cream and grilled bread with cheese. It's almost as if Grandma Patty knew this and our food arrives.

"Well, folks, be careful. Most of your plates are pretty hot." Everyone looks so happy and ready to eat. "Here's your salad, little lady. Two orders of pancakes for you two beautiful women. Your scrambled eggs, sweetheart. Anything else I can get you?"

Sarah takes the food quickly out of her hand. She's like a lion spotting a hyena. "Yes, some ketchup would be great and maybe some hot sauce!"

"You got it. Here's your breakfast burrito with extra bacon, fella. Here's your grilled cheese and taters, sweet cheeks. I'll be right back with your strawberry waffle."

I swear to whoever you worship there are rainbows shooting out of my grilled cheese. It looks like perfection. The mashed potatoes look like little clouds from heaven just waiting patiently to be eaten. I take a bite and decide right here and now that this is the best meal of my life. Hands down. I'm pretty sure everyone agrees with me because they're wolfing down theirs, too.

Sarah, in her always curious voice, looks at Maria and says, "Are you from the Philippines? What's it like being gay there? Did people accept you?" Sarah truly has no boundaries. But, she asks things in such an innocent way that you can't get mad at her.

Maria turns bright red like the ketchup bottle sitting across from me. "Yes, I was born there. I lived there until I was twenty-one. I didn't tell anyone I was gay until I moved to America. I wanted a new life."

Sarah's hands are shaking, and she's sweating a lot on her forehead. "There's something I've been wanting to tell everyone…"

Why is she so nervous? What's going on? Is she pregnant?

Lauren's still on her phone. She must be talking to her boyfriend, Luis. He's from Peru and they're so in love. It's grossly cute and I bet he's happy to be part of something so American as prom.

We all cough and she looks up. It's nice to see her face not backlit by her phone. "Hi, guys! Sorry, I was talking to Luis. What did I miss?"

Tiffany, looking a little frustrated, looks at Lauren, and clears her throat. "Ahem. Sarah here said she has something to share with the group."

Lauren's embarrassed now. "Oh, geez, I'm sorry. I feel awful. What is it, Sare Bear?"

Sarah gulps and moves her hair out of her eye, "Guys, I think I'm bisexual. I mean, there's this super cute girl in my history class, right? But, then when I go to P.E. Steve Peak's there and he's just as cute.

I've known I'm not straight ever since I watched *Titanic*. To this day, I still don't know who I'd choose. Jack or Rose is a difficult choice. Ya know? Sorry, I didn't tell you sooner. I was just trying to figure this all out."

I say, "No reason to be sorry, Sarah. We love you no matter what."

"Yeah, Sarah! You kick ass," Ben excitedly says.

Lauren goes in for a hug. "That's super great. I've always wanted a gay best friend. No joke. But uh, what does this mean for us?"

I roll my eyes. "Oh, Lauren, this is a big moment and all you can think about is yourself?"

I'm incredibly grateful for this talk about prom and sexuality. One side of me is thinking that we should be talking about the murder more. The other side of me is just wanting to be a teenage girl.

Sarah puts her hand on her forehead while her eyes dart around all of us, "I don't know! That's the problem! They're both so great in their own ways."

Tiffany says, "Well, if I were you, I'd choose the girl. You can go to the bathroom together and get dresses in the same color. However, I'm biased. I was gay before it was cool."

Sarah laughs. "I feel so much better now. I didn't know how or when to tell you, but I didn't want to show up for photos with a date that's a girl or something weird. I don't ever want to make you guys uncomfortable or something."

"I don't think you are capable of making us feel uncomfortable. You know we love you no matter what. Even if your date was an alien," I say.

She exhales and smiles. "I knew I could count on you all to understand and support me. Thank you."

"So, Lucy tell me everything. What does your dress look like?" Maria asks.

I just realized I never even looked for one. Lauren and Sarah asked me a while ago, and I decided to stay home and watch all the scary movies I could find. "Well, funny story. I don't have one yet. Up until a few hours ago, I didn't want to go."

Ben rushes to my defense. "Yeah, I don't even have my fancy outfit yet. Girls have the easy part. They just get to choose a dress and be done with it."

Lauren puts her hand up and looks at him. "Dude, you're ridiculous and not in a fun way. Being a girl is way harder because there are limited cute dresses that look good. I mean, I have shirts at home that range from small to extra-large and dresses are no exception. Then you have to find the right color. It's exhausting."

Maria chimes in, "Yes! You are so right. It's impossible to find a dress for our wedding. I mean, I was a size two somewhere and then at the next, I was sixteen. I don't get it."

Tiffany says, "Babe, you could wear a potato sack and I'd still want to marry every day of my life."

Sarah rolls her eyes. "Your love is gross. This isn't fair. Lucy and Ben have each other. Lauren and Luis have each other. Tiffany and Maria have each other. Am I supposed to wait the rest of my life for my Prince or Princess Charming?"

Listening to all their complaints raises my anxiety. I wouldn't call myself fat, but I wouldn't call myself skinny either. Most of the clothes I wear are a size 2x because I'd rather be comfortable than sucked in an extra-large, where I'm just boobs on a stick walking around. I'm always comparing my body to mom's. She lived on nothing but cigarettes, vodka, gummy worms, and black coffee. She was so tiny. I bought almost every one of our groceries from Smiles and she was on a new diet almost every week. I am so ugly.

"Earth to Lucy, are you there?" Lauren asks.

"Yeah, I'm here. Sorry. I was just thinking of how small my mom is and how fat I am."

Tiffany puts her fork down and says, "Lucy. Don't ever think you're fat. Your mom drank a lot of her calories, but that doesn't mean she was healthy. Tequila and cigarettes aren't a diet."

"Yeah, I know. But, she was always calling me fat. I just feel like I'm nothing but boobs and a double chin."

Ben says, "She called you fat because she was insecure. It probably made her feel better putting you down. She doesn't matter."

I snap back to reality and everyone's still talking about prom and discussing what color dress they're going to wear. Surprise, surprise. Lauren's taking this whole thing so seriously. I feel like her future wedding day won't compare to the anxiety she seems to have. It's weird. I'm also worried she's not breathing.

"So, yeah, my dress is going to be purple, of course. I am also thinking that we should take a limo. We would look so cool showing up in one!"

"Wait, stop right there. A limo? Isn't that a little extreme?" Ben asks.

Lauren says, "Well, yeah. But how many Proms are we ever going to have in our lives. Ya know?"

Frantically, I get up and tell everyone, "I'm going to run to the bathroom. I'll be back."

Before I hear their responses, I run to the bathroom and into the nearest stall. I plop down on the white shiny toilet seat without pulling down my leggings, even though they feel more constricted than usual.

My entire body changes from tingly to tense every few seconds as I sit here. It needs to make up its mind. I feel like I'm about to vomit. I can't take any deep breaths, and the bathroom tiles have merged into one blue image. It reminds me of a kaleidoscope held up to my eye. I feel like I'm freezing and wish I'd brought a jacket with me.

I get up, leave the stall, and splash some water on my face. Before I dry my face, I run back into the stall because I am for sure going to throw up.

I pull my brown hair back just in time. My grilled cheese, waffles, and pie are all wanting to leave my body as quickly as they entered. I leave quite a mess in the toilet bowl. My mouth tastes like stomach acid, maple syrup, and regret for eating so much.

I slowly get up after making sure nothing is left and walk to the sink. I splash more cold water on my face and look in the mirror. I'm glad I didn't get any throw up in my hair or on my shirt. I like this shirt, even though Snowball's fur's all over it. It's the Glitter Tooth shirt I bought at their show last year in Tucson.

I try to remind myself of a familiar mantra.

My bipolar doesn't define me.

My bipolar doesn't define me.

I open the bathroom door, and Tiffany's there, waiting. She looks worried.

"Lucy, you okay? What happened?"

What should I say? I don't want to lie to her. She's my only family now, after all. If we're going to get to know each other, lying probably won't be the best way to go about it.

I try to maintain eye contact, but Tiffany only has one eye with everything swirling. "No, I'm not. I'm beyond depressed about all this. I usually talk to my therapist who helps me out with my mental health and stuff. But, lately with everything being so crazy, I haven't been able to. Besides the bipolar and I PTSD. Just a few seconds ago, I was pretty sure I was dying."

"Oh, Lucy, I'm so sorry. I, too, have PTSD. My ex-husband came after me with a knife and I've never been the same. It does get easier though, with time. You aren't dying. You were having a panic attack. I had my first one when I was nine. Repeat after me, I'm not dying."

"I'm not dying. Is everyone okay? Are they mad at me? Wait, ex-husband? Is there something I'm missing here?"

She rolls her eyes and giggles. "Yes, everyone's okay. They're just worried about you and not mad at all. Yes, I've been married to a man before. It was a dark time and a story for later. Do you need a hug?"

A hug sounds nice. But, so does a new life. Better yet, a one-way ticket to Japan where no one knows me. Obviously, that's not possible. I gotta snap out of it.

I slowly go in for a hug. "Thank you. I'm glad you're here. I don't know what to do. I mean she was my mom. Ya know?"

She shakes her head. "Oh, Lucy, I want you to remember this. This isn't your permanent and everything that's happening with your mom isn't your fault. Kelly's been mentally ill for as long as I can remember and I guess her brain finally just gave in to her demons. You'll get through this. You have many people to lean on, including Maria and me now. Let's go back, drink some water, and plan your last high school dance."

As I walk to the table, all I can think of is how much I want my brain to stop and that I don't want to go to school or work this week. Is your mom murdering someone and going to jail a valid excuse for time off?

Ben and I make eye contact. Sometimes I wish we could speak telepathically. It would make things way easier. He gets up from the booth and kisses me firmly on the lips.

Sarah sarcastically says, "Oh, get a room you two! That's gross." If only she knew how good it felt to have his lips touch mine. It sent a shiver down my spine all the way to my feet.

"Doing better, LL?" Lauren asks. That's the most genuine she's sounded all day.

I look down at my feet to make sure they're still on the ground. All this anxiety has made me feel like I'm floating. I vibrate with nerves. "Yeah, I'm okay. I just needed some water."

Maria looks up from the check that Patty brought while I was gone. "Welcome back, honey. We missed you."

"Did I miss anything?"

Ben says, "Lucy, we've all been talking, and there's something I've been meaning to ask you."

"Okay… Yeah? What is it?" Why's my heart fluttering? It's not like he's going to propose or something. This is a strange feeling.

"Will you go to prom with me? You'd make me the happiest guy in the world." His smile's the biggest one I've ever seen him have.

I notice the table next to us isn't empty anymore. It looks like he gathered all the ketchup bottles, sugar packets, silverware, and coffee cups he could find in the restaurant, and spelled out PROM? I giggle awkwardly. "Why yes, Benjamin. I'd be honored."

I swear to God Lauren and Sarah are crying, and the whole restaurant, including Patty, are clapping. What has my life become?

After much reassurance that they "got it", Maria and Tiffany pay the bill. I feel bad about it, but I'll pay them back soon. I have that cash from grandpa in my room.

"Save money for college next year and memories You kids are in high school," Maria says.

Ben looks relieved and his shoulders drop a little. He's been saving up for when we drive to Seattle. Out-of-state tuition is going to suck a lot for both of us.

Before we leave the table, Patty comes over one last time. "Thanks, folks. I hope y'all have a great night and hope to see you soon. It's been an absolute pleasure being your waitress this evening."

All together we say, "Thank you, Patty! It was all delicious."

Lauren slaps my butt like she sometimes does just to be funny. "So, Lucy, I know this all sucks. But, try and remember how strong you are."

Sarah adds, "You'll be at school on Monday, right?"

I put my arms around them. "No, probably not. I'm thinking I'll come back on Wednesday. I just want to be around Snowball for a while."

Mid-sentence, Ben stops talking to Tiffany and Maria about the current crisis of children in Palestine. "Uh, hello? Boyfriend right here?"

Shit. I scramble for words that will help him feel important, which he is. "You don't count! You're my warrior! My every breath! My beating heart!"

He laughs. "Oh, Lucy. I'm just messing with you. I know you didn't forget about me. I mean, how could you? Have you met me?"

I swear that dude could make me laugh even if we were on a crashing airplane. I sometimes wish he'd go into comedy or something less serious than bringing peace to the Middle East, but I don't want to stop his dreams. I roll my eyes for what feels like the hundredth time tonight.

"Yes, I've met you and am actually very much in love with you. Are you ready to go home and face Chuck?"

He thinks for a few seconds. "No. What other choice do we have?"

We walk Lauren and Sarah to the blue car, give them big hugs, and they make me promise to text them tomorrow.

Sarah squeezes me tight. "Lucy, you better text me the second you wake up or I'm going to be super upset."

Lauren nods. "Yeah, Luce, you gotta keep us in the loop. We got your back now and always." She turns the car on and immediately Glitter Tooth's hit "Heart Autopsy" blasts.

I can't help but sing along. Maria and Tiffany join in too, and we have a full-on singing and dancing party in the middle of the parking lot. Ben's even doing the robot. He's such a weirdo.

The song's over and Lauren blows kisses at us. "It's way past my curfew. I gotta race home after I drop Sarah off. Love you all. Especially you, Lucy. See you soon!"

As they speed off, the radio turns into a quiet hum. Maria and Tiffany walk over to the red convertible hand-in-hand. I hear crickets as my heart beats fast. The sky is as dark as coffee grounds and I search for another shooting star.

I look at Ben and say, "I was thinking tomorrow you, me, Snowball, stupid horror movies and pizza? Sounds good?"

He winks. "Of course. I can't wait to yell at the screen as people make stupid decisions. They always lead them right to the killer."

"Well, not everyone can be as smart as you."

Maria and Tiffany flash the bright headlights at us, and Tiffany says, "You need a ride?"

On the way home, I feel myself getting more nervous by the second. Then literally over ten thoughts enter my head. Why did I eat so much? Who can I trust right now? What's Chuck going to say? Will he hit me too? Do I tell him? Does he already know? What's Mom doing? Is she okay? What does prison food taste like? Is her cellmate nice? Wait, do murderers get cellmates?

My hands feel like I've been swimming all day. The sweat from anxiety and frustration coming out on my clenching fists have made them clammy and raisin-y.

The drive seems a lot quicker than on the way there. I see our dark-blue door. I hope Snowball's safe and Chuck's sleeping. He deserves some rest.

"Lucy, do you want Maria and me to go inside with you? I have the cops on speed dial now and we'll be your bodyguards. I have a black belt in karate. Did I ever tell you that?" Tiffany says it like it's no big deal.

"Aren't her arms the best? Look at how strong she is. I could touch them all day. She can kick anyone's ass."

Tiffany blushes. "Babe, don't put me on the spot like that. You know I get embarrassed."

Ben clears his throat. "Sorry to stop whatever's going on here, but we need to go take care of this stuff with Chuck before it blows up into something worse. Are you ready?"

With a new sense of confidence, I feel ready to go. My heart races and my muscles are tense, but I turn it into energy. I'm unstoppable with their support. I look at the three of them, a little anxious but okay.

I nod my head, "Yes, I'm great. Let's do this shit."

I open my green purse, push aside my yellow flowered wallet, and pull out my yellow and green pineapple lanyard. I have my house keys, a spare key to my mom's 1998 black sedan that's falling apart, and the keys for all the doors at Smiles.

I slowly close the convertible's door to make sure I don't wake up any of the nosy neighbors. Everyone's behind me and going at the same slow pace. I'm glad for this. The last thing I want to feel is rushed.

I let everyone shuffle in and put my pointer finger on my lips, making sure they all get the hint that we need to be as quiet as possible.

Ben stands in the doorway with me so he can hold my hand. Tiffany and Maria both hunch down and look like a big black sheet against the side of the door.

Luckily, I don't hear Chuck yet, but there are some artifacts that definitely show me he's here. Empty beer cans, Chinese takeout containers soaked full of soy sauce. And his wallet's open with all his credit cards and coins spilling everywhere.

CHAPTER EIGHT

He's snoring in his recliner and Snowball's on his lap. The TV, stuck on old sports reruns, leaves a glow on her fur. It almost looks like a body halo. She's such a precious little being.

I walk over to them slowly while Ben, Maria, and Tiffany go to my room. I want to cuddle Snowball and let Chuck keep sleeping. She jumps off the gray recliner, slams to the ground, circles my legs, and looks up at me meowing. I hear some groans.

Shit.

"Kelly, is that you, baby?"

Gross. Who calls someone baby? I hate when people call their partner names that aren't related to their first name. It has never made sense to me. I quietly pick up Snowball and put her in the room. I come back into the living room with Chuck.

"Kelly? Where did you go?" Chuck's off the recliner and peering into the fridge now. My bet is he's looking for more beer.

I sit at the kitchen table that's still full of makeup. "Hey, sit down. We gotta talk."

"Lucy? I didn't even know you were here. You scared the shit out of me. I called your mom a bunch of times. What the fuck's going on? Where is she? Her car's still here."

He needs to slow down if this is going to work. I take two deep breaths.

"Sit down, please. There's a lot we need to talk about."

Chuck turns on the kitchen light and pulls up a chair. I was right. He has a beer in his hand. "Okay, I'm sitting down. Please tell me where she is. I'm tired of these games."

I clench my fists and swallow my pride. "Listen, dude, my mom's not coming back for a while, probably not ever."

Chuck slams his beer on the table. He leans towards me and I notice a vein in his neck starting to poke out. I hear the door to my room open and Ben walks into the kitchen and sits down next to me. He unclenches my fist and replaces it with his soft, powerful hand.

He looks Chuck in the eyes. "Kelly's not coming back. We've had a super long day and don't deserve you getting mad at us."

Chuck stands up and walks back to the fridge to get more beer. He's going hard on the alcohol, it seems. I haven't seen him drink this much since his birthday.

He lets out a gross burp and tells us, "Will someone start making sense? All I'm asking is where Kelly is. I was at the bars all night and no one said they'd seen her. This is weird behavior. Even for her."

I put my hands on the table. "She's in jail, dude. She killed your dad. Mick Kane and his officers came to question her, she apparently admitted to murder."

Chuck, who's now about four beers deep says, "Wait, what? You mean to tell me Kelly— You're pulling my chain, Lucy. We both know Kelly would never do that. I know she hated him, but— Besides, she wouldn't even know how to shoot a soda can if it was right in front of her face."

My door slams and the noise echoes through the entire house. I hear high heels coming down the hallway. Tiffany walks into the kitchen and sits down. Her face is super red and full of sweat.

She looks Chuck in the eyes and seriously looks like she's about to punch him. "Listen, asshole, you better not be making threats to my niece. She has nothing to do with any of this."

Chuck chokes on his next words. "What? Listen, I'm not making any threats. I'm just in complete shock. Nothing seems to make sense. Kelly hated my dad, but I never thought it'd turn into murder."

Tiffany says, "I don't think any of us thought this was a possibility. Yeah, my sister is a little crazy and would benefit from some kind of medication. I probably should've been there more for her, too."

Chuck crosses his arms. "Yeah, she probably would've done a lot better with family. I mean I've been her, for, what? Ten years? She's always extra crazy on holidays. Family might've helped her drink less. I took in Lucy as my own. I mean the kid looked like she didn't sleep when I first met her. I had to do something."

I sarcastically say, "Thank you, King Chuck. I didn't know I was such a chore."

"You know what I mean, LL. I've been there for you since you were knee-high and it's not like your mom and you are the easiest people to deal with."

Tiffany clears her throat. "Well, I'm glad we can admit that Kelly is a little crazy. Despite the craziness, we need to find a way to keep her safe somehow. Maybe get her a lawyer."

Chuck inhales another beer and says, "Can we slow down a little? My brain is trying to grasp the fact that the love of my life killed my father. No, you guys want me to be there for her more?"

Wow. It's all real now. My mom's in jail. The next time I see her, she'll probably be in orange or some kind of weird jail uniform. I can't believe she won't be in high heels or any makeup. I think this will be one of the few times in my life where she isn't all dolled up.

Tiffany gets up and gives Chuck a side hug, "Dude, don't beat yourself up about this. We all know how stubborn she is. Kelly was going to kill him no matter what. There's nothing anyone could have done or said to change her mind."

Ben looks at me and reminds me, "The longest and worst day's over. Tomorrow, I hope your mom calls so we get more answers and can find a way to help her. But, let's try and get some sleep."

"I agree, but I need to stay up a little bit longer to make sure Chuck is okay. Go play with your Pez or something. I'll be in there soon."

He kisses my cheek, "Okay. Just don't stay up too late. We have a long day of movies tomorrow."

Ben walks to our room with Snowball prancing right behind him. I say, "Okay, Chuck, let's try and figure out a few things. I bet the lawyer is going to have a few questions. Like, how did she obtain the gun?"

"Well, all of my personal belongings are in my safe. She doesn't know the code, so that's out of the question."

I roll my eyes. "Your safe probably isn't even locked. Let's be real here. You aren't the smartest person with privacy. I mean, remember when my mom figured out your bank password and stole one hundred dollars from you? Good times. I bet I could even figure out your safe code."

Chuck says, "I bet you fifty dollars you won't be able to. I'll give you three guesses. Starting now."

This will be easy. He's not the smartest with keeping his things private. If I were him, I'd probably make it the year I was born. He's forty so I'm going to guess 1980. But I'll make up the first two, so he doesn't feel so bad about his lack of security.

I turn my head to face him. "Okay, is it zero, zero, zero, zero?"

"No, LL. What do you take me for, a total idiot?"

I wish I could say yes, but I don't want to be entirely rude. "How about something straightforward like one, two, three, four?"

He sighs and sticks out his tongue. "No, Lucy, get real. I'm not in kindergarten anymore."

I put my hand out. "Sorry, buddy. I know it's 1980."

His jaw drops, and he smacks the table with his hand. "Fuck you, Lucy! How did you— Did you cheat or something?"

"How could I cheat? It's not my fault that you're just easy to figure out."

Tiffany laughs, "Come on, dude. Don't ever make things your birth year! It's so easy to figure out. We'll reprogram it tomorrow. Okay?"

Chuck's eyes start to flicker, "Yes, tomorrow. Waking up without Kelly is going to suck. At least when she was at friend's houses, I knew she'd be coming back. But, not this time." He starts bawling. His mouth opens, but no words want to come out. He's like me a few hours ago.

I say, "We'll get through this together. You're the dad I always wanted. Now, it's time for us to act like a family. With or without mom."

Chuck pulls me close, "Yes, we'll get through this. Daughter."

My heart swells with him calling me daughter. Mom always called me baby girl, monkey, or some other random nickname she could think of. I've never been called that until this very moment. Well, there were times when creepy men would ask if mom and I were sisters. She'd eventually tell them that I was her daughter, but that was way after they had bought her a drink. Or two.

I never thought that it would take mom murdering someone for me to feel like this. Like I have a place in this world. A place that goes beyond Arizona.

A family. People who love me more than alcohol.

I'm looking through my white clothes hamper for something to sleep in. Something that will make me feel free and not bound by fabric. I eventually find one of Ben's 3x shirts with the periodic table on it.

I pass his Pez collection, and I can't help but feel incredibly lucky to have him in my life. I mean, who else would collect random Pez dispensers? Only Ben. Still, my life feels like it's falling apart. This has truly been the day from hell and all I want is for things to be back to normal.

Tiffany knocks and says, "Can I come in? I need to get Maria, so we can get to sleep."

Maria who's admiring all of the Glitter Tooth memorabilia in my room says, "Come on in. I'm just looking at stuff."

Tiffany gives me a hug, "Proud of you kiddo. If this was me, I'd be in full freak out mode. You're definitely a fighter. You got that from your grandpa. Until his last breath, he kept going. Thinking he could still drive."

Maria laughs, "Yep, Dean insisted that he could drive to get ice cream for us. It took a lot of nudging for him to realize that he could barely see over the steering wheel."

Ben says, "Yeah, that definitely sounds like Lucy. She is always trying to overexert herself or be there for people no matter what. Even if she's not feeling good."

I shove him, "Don't be telling my secrets. They don't need to know everything yet."

Out of nowhere, my body feels tight. Almost like a bodybuilder. my arms are flexing without me trying. It feels like a huge snake is wrapped around me while I gasp for air.

While I struggle to breathe, I come to the conclusion that not existing and not having to deal with any of these problems and people sounds perfect.

I turn to everyone, announcing, "I'm going to take a shower and climb into bed. I'll see you guys later. Love you."

I squeeze my fist in the middle of the hallway, Tiffany says, "Wait, Lucy. Before you go, Maria and I want to have a little bit of a memorial for my dad tomorrow. Nothing too formal. He's already cremated. We just want to have a little bit of a goodbye. What do you think?"

"Yeah, that sounds like a good idea. I'd love to. I'm sorry we couldn't do it with mom."

"It's okay, Lucy. It's better than nothing. Maria and I are going to figure out the details. Love you."

"Love you, too."

I find my green palm tree beach towel in the hallway closet and hear Ben talking to Tiffany and Maria.

"There are some sleeping bags in here. You guys can sleep on the floor in the living room if you want. Or you can go back to your hotel. Whatever sounds best to you guys."

Maria tells Ben, "As much as I want to stay here, I think we should stay at the hotel tonight. Lucy needs time alone."

I smile because I'm grateful everyone knows that being alone is what I need. Well, not fully alone. Ben, Snowball, and stupid horror movies will be with me, obviously.

I turn on the shower and put my green palm tree beach towel on the toilet. The steam fogging up my vision and covering my feet feels so good on my skin. I open my sea salt body wash, lather it on my skin, and all my troubles are now on pause. The thoughts of my mom being in jail, Chuck being the worst, and what my future holds are going down the drain just like the bubbles. I want to stay here forever.

I look to the right through my clear shower curtain for a second and see how pitch black it is outside. The bathroom light creates a perfect silhouette of the moon. Snowball's sitting on top of my towel, and she meows at me. I think she misses me. She's developed a little bit of separation anxiety from Ben and me since we adopted her a few weeks ago.

"Snowball, come here, girl. Mom wants some alone time," Ben says.

She jumps off the toilet and scampers back to the room. Reality hit me again. I need to calm down. Color exercise begin.

I see a white wall.

I see a green shampoo bottle.

I see my tan wrinkled hands from being in the shower for too long. They look like raisins.

I turn the water off and sit down on the wet beige tile. I take deep breaths so my heartbeat might slow down. I wish I could magically erase my anxiety. It's making everything feel one hundred times worse. Deep breaths, Lucy. You'll get through this. Happy thoughts. Think of Snowball, cheese pizza, gray rain clouds, watermelon bubblegum, belly laughs, chocolate ice cream, and orange sunsets.

I open the shower door, dry off, and put my pajamas on. Back in my bedroom where Ben and Snowball are, I take my meds. I feel a little better. I have some good people on my side and my mom's definitely going to call me tomorrow. I can't wait.

Ben's already lying down with Snowball, and they're watching cat videos on my laptop. I give them each a kiss goodnight and roll over. My head's full of a million thoughts, but I let the kitten meows sing me to sleep.

Tomorrow's going to be better.

I wake up with a strong craving for cereal. I hope we have some. Ben's still snoring and Snowball is sprawled out between us. I want to keep sleeping, but there's too much going on in my brain. I want to make sure I'm awake to answer my mom's phone call. I wish I could tilt my head and have all my thoughts come out my ears so I don't feel like I'm constantly juggling everything.

I make sure I have my phone, kiss Ben on the forehead, and go to the kitchen. The sink's full of empty beer bottles, rib bones soaked in barbecue sauce, a bunch of my mom's gummy worm packages, and chili cans. I know Chuck is grieving or whatever, so he gets a pass this time. I open the dishwasher and take out a red bowl. Luckily, it's clean. There's a halo of soap residue on some of the bowls, though.

We have Tasty O's! I pour the delicious fruit-flavored circles in the bowl and drown them in almond milk. I open my *Time Travelers from Mars* book and start reading. I'm at the part where the time travelers finally try deep-dish pizza.

My phone rings, displaying a Phoenix area code. I don't know anyone there, but I answer anyway. A robotic voice says, "You have a collect call from Arizona State Holding Cell in Perryville. Do you accept the charges?"

"Yes, of course!"

A familiar voice comes on the line. My mom, out of breath, speaks, "Lucy, is that you?"

I roll my eyes. "Of course it is. But hi, Mom! Hi! Are you okay?"

"Yes, baby girl, it's me. I only have two minutes, so we gotta make this quick. The other girls here are gonna fight me to use the phone if I don't hurry."

"Okay. How are you? Are the people nice to you?"

"I'm fine. Everyone's wanting to come up with an escape plan soon. I just want some Golden Gaucho cigarettes and gummy worms. Will you send me some? They said I can get mail sometimes."

"Yeah… I guess so. What's the address there?"

"It's 1627 Desert Drive, Phoenix. I don't know the zip code. Look it up on your phone, I guess. How's Chuck?"

"He's fine. He misses you. We all miss you!"

"I miss you guys, too. Be sure to send me that stuff, okay? My time's up. Bye, baby girl!"

"Mom, wait…" She hung up. She's not there. Complete silence. I didn't even get to say goodbye. I guess family can break your heart. I don't even want Tasty O's anymore. I'm so upset and annoyed that this is my life. Tears stream down my face and I feel like I'm dying. I hate crying.

I don't want to be alone right now. Ben's still sleeping with Snowball and I don't want to call anyone. I'm positive Lauren or Sarah would come over, but I don't want to be seen like this. I walk back to my bedroom and crawl in the warm and messy bed with Ben and pull him close to my body.

He wakes up suddenly. "Lucy, what's up?" He seems a little scared and out of breath.

I can't form any thoughts, I'm so sad. I'm still crying a little try to find the right words. "I'm not doing so well. I just got off the phone with my mom." He turns to face me and pulls me closer. Snowball jumps off the bed since she tends to get upset if she gets woken up. Ben knows something's wrong—he always knows.

"What's going on, Luce? Wanna talk about it?"

I don't. I always feel like an inconvenience to people, if I complain about my problems. Even talking to my therapist, it's like I'm annoying her. I even ask how she's doing. like a need to make sure no one ever sees me sad. I just play the role of happy Lucy. Who no one ever has to worry about. I need to push myself. Every time I do talk about myself and explain more about what's going on, I always feel better.

I take a deep breath and avoid eye contact. "My mom called me. It didn't go as well as I wanted."

Ben looks concerned. He sits up a little and rubs his eyes. "What happened? Is your mom alright? How's jail going? I still can't believe all this is happening. She's going to go crazy without lipstick or gummy worms."

I sit up too and drink some water. "She sounded fine. She said she only had two minutes to talk and asked me to send her stuff. And—"

Ben interrupts me, "Wait, she called you to ask for things? Can she even get things in jail? Two minutes? That's way too quick of a phone call."

"I know, right? I don't even think it was two minutes, honestly. I don't want to send her anything. She didn't even ask how I was at all."

He steals my phone. "I'm going to check if you guys even talked for two minutes. I'm sorry, Lucy. Your mom's consistently selfish, so I mean, we can't expect too much from her, I guess." I was right. We only talked for about one minute and ten seconds. I'm not even worth a whole two minutes, I guess. She sucks.

"Get out of bed, McBride. We're making today our bitch. No more pity parties. I'm not letting you stay in bed feeling sorry for yourself. We also are going to celebrate your grandpa today, right?"

I turn over and put my pillow over my head. "I don't want to do anything, though. I just want to sleep all day and wake up with everything back to the way that it was."

"I'm going to squeeze all the sadness out of you." Ben reaches under the covers and hugs me so tight I can barely breathe. "Your mom doesn't deserve any of your attention anymore. She's behind bars. Don't let her drag you in there, too." My chest hurts a little from the squeezing.

I giggle from his silliness but still feel sad. "Thanks. I'll need a more of those. I can't help but feel sad, though. She's the only family I've known."

CHAPTER NINE

B en pinches my arm and smirks. "Stop saying things that aren't true!"

"Ouch, dude! What was that for?"

He rolls his eyes and pushes his hair away from his face. "Lucy, you have a family. You have me and Snowball. You also have Tiffany, Maria, Lauren, and Sarah. That's way more than some people can say."

"But what about my mom? What's going to happen to her? Or Chuck? Are we still going to move out of here?"

"Yes, of course. That hasn't changed. Just breathe. I need something to eat. Do we have any cereal? Sorry, I need fuel for today."

We go into the kitchen, and I pull the Tasty O's out of the cupboard. "I was so excited this morning to smell their fruity goodness when I woke up. But, I wasn't able to finish because of the call with my mom."

He sees the bowl of cereal on the counter I took maybe two bites of. The Tasty O's look droopy and sad like wilted flowers. The milk must be warm by now.

"Yours? We both know you can eat way more than that."

I hate wasting food but my soggy remains are a little pink and looks gross. I dump it down the drain. "Well, what're we doing today, Benjamin?"

He sticks his almond milk in the freezer. He only drinks milk in his cereal if it's super cold. He refuses to drink milk that's just a little bit warm. It drives me crazy, especially when I make cookies and he waits to eat one with his milk.

Ben focuses on his socks. "Well, I did something… But you have to agree that you won't get mad at me." My heart paces. What could he have done? He looks at me. "Well, I texted Lauren and Sarah earlier and said they should pick you up for a girls' day. Maybe go get your prom dress. Don't kill me."

Sigh. He had me worried. I give him a hug. But, hanging out with friends? I know I sound ungrateful, but I don't want people to see me when I feel like this.

"Wait, isn't today Monday? How are they taking the day off from school?"

"They are taking the day off to make sure your dress gets taken care of. Don't worry, I called for us, too. I said you're sick. The office lady probably knows the truth, but whatever. Please don't kill me. I was just trying to help."

"I'm not going to kill you. I'm upset because I wanted to sleep all day. What about watching horror movies together? Is that not happening anymore? What about Snowball? Who will she hang out with?"

He grabs my hands. "Lucy, don't drag the cat into this. She'll be just fine without you. She likes us only half the time anyway, especially when we give her food. Also, we own so many horror movies on DVD so that comment is ridiculous because obviously they aren't going anywhere. Just go hang out with your friends. Snowball and I will be here when you get back. You're going to look so beautiful in your dress. I love you."

I always blush when he says that. I kiss his cheek. "I love you too, Ben. I just don't want to be around anyone today. Oops! What about my grandpa's memorial? And you know how much I hate trying things on in dressing rooms."

"We are going to do your grandpa's memorial when you all come home. Also, the dressing rooms are not scary. You are beautiful."

I hate dressing rooms. I'm no size two and never will be. I don't ever say no to French fries and find it almost impossible to find clothes that fit or that I like. The last time I went to the mall, I saw leggings with donuts on them and jean overalls with flowers which seemed to me like a second grader decorated them. I was there for fifteen minutes and that was enough. I decided to get a soft pretzel and I got a poetry book with the money my mom stole from Chuck. When she came to pick me up, we shopped for her instead. She found boots, dresses, and all kinds of earrings. We told Chuck some of it was for me, but he knew better.

"Well, what time are they going to be here? Do I at least have time to be alone for a little?"

Ben, who's finally taken his milk out of the freezer, pours himself a bowl of cereal. "Yes, of course. They'll be here at one o'clock. You have a few hours. Just breathe, Lucy. They're not going to hurt you. You're safe."

I give him a hug and head to the bedroom. I lie down and check my phone.

I open my group text thread with Sarah and Lauren, *"Well, the secret's out. Ben told me you guys are coming over, I guess."*

Sarah responds right away, *"Yay! I'm glad I didn't have to keep it much longer. See you soon! Look online for ideas!"*

Lauren texts back as well, *"We're going to have so much fun! I can't wait. See you girls, soon!"*

I put my phone down and just want to close my eyes to take a nap for a little bit before the chaos begins. Snowball jumps on the bed and puts her butt right in my face. Maybe it's a sign I shouldn't be back in bed.

Ben screams from the kitchen, "Lucy, what're you doing in there? You better not be sleeping."

I open my eyes. "How the fuck do you always know? I'm just taking a power nap."

He runs down the hallway, jumps in the bed, and cuddles up next to me. "If you don't take a nap, I'll make you a grilled cheese," he whispers.

Ben doesn't know how to boil water, but his grilled cheese making abilities are out of this world. It's my biggest comfort food. I always buy cheese at Smiles, so our fridge is full of at least two different kinds. White cheddar and pepper jack are my personal favorites. Most emotional breakdowns or bad grades can be healed with soft cheese and warm bread.

I take my pills and decide to turn my Glitter Tooth playlist on. The main singer, Allison Zee, has a voice that could cure any alignment. Combine that with her lyrics and you have the best combination ever. I sing along with Allison.

"One day I was young
I thought I knew it all
But, now I realize I don't know anything
Always forward, never backward
Missing those childhood days
Where nothing mattered
Always forward, never backward"

Singing along always makes me feel less alone. Chuck introduced me to Glitter Tooth when we first met. They were super popular in the 80's, but that hasn't stopped my obsession. I smell the cheese in the kitchen. I'm so hungry, I could eat a shoe. I should get dressed first, though. Since, I'll be trying on clothes all day, I'm going to find the comfiest clothes I have. Ones that make me feel good and not fat.

"Lucy, your sandwich is ready!" Ben calls from the kitchen.

"Be right there!"

One more visual exercise before I face everyone and must be social.

I see my purple sheets.

I see my white unicorn stuffed animal Ben won for me at the fair last summer. He's always so good at those impossible carnival games.

I see my cat's doing yoga poses on the wall. This month it's an orange cat named Marmalade.

I hear Tiffany and Maria. Tiffany says, "Yeah, I agree. Lucy is stronger than she thinks." I spot my sandwich. It's cut in half just the way I like it. I take a huge bite of the melted cheesy goodness. It's perfect.

Mid bite, I say, "Thank you, Ben. This is exactly what I needed."

Maria says, "Good to see you smiling, Lucy. How are you today?"

"I'm alright. I'm not looking forward to today that much. Oh, I forgot! My mom called this morning."

Tiffany, who's talking to Ben, must have overheard me. She runs over on the green-tiled kitchen floor. "Oh, honey, how was that? That must have been nice hearing from her."

I shrug my shoulders. "It sucked. We talked for a minute, but she didn't ask how I was. I try to understand her selfishness and all. I mean, growing up with a difficult dad like you guys had couldn't have been easy. I mean, you know that especially, Tiffany."

Tiffany's eyes dilate and says, "What're you talking about, Lucy? Yes, my dad had a temper, but he loved us so much. When he kicked your mom out, I know he tried to connect with her for years. He even thought of you enough to write a card with money in his signature green envelopes. He only used those for special occasions."

I freeze. "Wait, what? I've heard nothing but bad things all the freaking time about him. He did kick my mom out before I was born, right? That doesn't seem too saint-y to me."

Tiffany crosses her arms. "Kelly left on her own terms. She was hanging out with men twice her age before you were born. Lucy, your grandpa always sent her money to support you growing up. How do you think you got school supplies? She never worked a day in her life."

Could Tiffany be right? But I remember my mom working at a Circle K gas station when I was a kid. She picked me up after school in her tan work shirt with the huge K on it and faded khakis. She always smelled like alcohol, vanilla perfume, and mint gum. She told me all about her day and always had such elaborate stories about customers. Were those lies?

"Lucy, I know you constantly want to stand up for your mom and I hate that she's brainwashed you into thinking she's done so much for you. But sweetie, she's incredibly selfish. She always has been. Part of the reason your grandpa was so upset when she got pregnant was because your mom could barely take care of herself. We were all worried about how she'd even manage a baby."

I start to feel incredibly conflicted. A part of me knows that she was selfish, but it's not all her fault. She was young when she had me, so she didn't know what she was doing. I mean she also didn't have anyone around that cared about her. No one's perfect.

I put my fists on my side and turn to Tiffany. "Well, if she's so awful, why the fuck did you come down to see her? I wanted my mom, Ben, and me to get out of Arizona and just move to Seattle. But no, you came here and screwed everything up."

I don't know if this burst of upset is bipolar based. Regardless, I'm so angry, I feel like I'm about to explode. My brain's full of so many thoughts, but I mostly understand why mom kicked Tiffany and Maria out of the house. They don't know what they're talking about. I don't even want to go shopping anymore. I didn't in the first place.

Now, I'm trying my best to calm down and nothing's working.

Ben looks at me. "Lucy, take some deep breaths. Your mom being selfish isn't any kind of breakthrough. You've known this for quite some time. Do you want some green tea? I'll put some honey in it. Try the color thing your therapist lady taught you."

Maria avoids eye contact and has her arms folded into her chest. "Uh, Lucy, I think Ben's right. Let's all do this color thing. What's it supposed to do?"

I'm not mad at Maria. She hasn't done anything wrong. I say, "I start pointing out colors in my head. When I get overwhelmed. It's supposed to make me more centered, or whatever."

Tiffany raises her hand. "Can I do it too? Only if it's okay with you, Luce. I'm overwhelmed. I don't want you to be mad at me."

I look at the floor. She's the only blood family I have left. I'm still mad at her, though. She can't just come in here and say all these hurtful things about mom. She barely knew her.

"Yeah, I guess you can do it. Don't think you're off the hook, though. I'm still very mad at you."

Ben leads us to the couch, and we sit. "I'll start," he says. "I see Snowball, the cutest white kitty sleeping. I see red lipstick still on the table. I see Lucy's beautiful brown eyes. You're next, Lucy."

I knew he'd pick me. "I see Ben's blue eyes. I see my purple flats on the floor. I see Chuck's yellow and red Arizona Cardinals lanyard. You're up, Maria."

Maria sits up straighter. "I see Tiffany's blonde hair. I see a green wall. I see Lucy as a little girl in a yellow bathing suit in that picture frame. Guess you're last, babe."

Maria winks at Tiffany, and Tiffany tells us, "I see Maria's blue jean jacket. I see Kelly's neon-colored gummy packets all over the house. I see Lucy in a black T-shirt, who I want to hug."

"Please, please, don't hug me. I just want to melt away and have this all be a nightmare I'm going to wake up from soon. Can we have a deal that we just don't talk about this until we get home later? I'm already not excited about today. I don't want to be thinking of bullshit all day, too. I also don't want Lauren and Sarah involved in all of this family stuff."

I put my hand out for Tiffany to shake in an agreement not to talk about it for a little bit, but of course, she hugs me. Well, I think tackle would be a better word. She and Maria hug me from both sides making a Lucy sandwich.

Maria pulls away and gives me a kiss on my cheek. "Ya know, Lucy, you have your grandpa's eyes and dimples. He had a big brain. Never knew what he was thinking."

Ben laughs. "That's something they also have in common. Half the time, I don't know what she's thinking. It must be a McBride thing."

Tiffany clears her throat. "Kelly and I didn't get that. We had a very outspoken mother. She'd tell anyone every detail about her dinner the night before if the right person was willing to listen."

"Will you tell me more about her later? I'd like to know because maybe she has some similar qualities to mom and I can understand her more. This all sucks. I'm tired of feeling shitty."

Tiffany gives me a kind of smile, "I hate everything going on as much as you. I came here to reconnect with you and your mom. In my wildest dreams, I never thought she'd be a murderer. But, what I do know is I love you and life's seldom easy or the way we want it to be."

Why does she have to be right? My life has never felt easy, but can't it be for just a little bit? I deserve that much. God or whoever's up there, if you're hearing this, send me a message. Give me a sign it'll get easier or better. It has to, right? One person shouldn't have to feel this sad and overwhelmed by life all the time.

Lauren and Sarah are at the door. I hear their giggles from here. I run to give myself a few seconds of alone time before the craziness of the day. Ben's usually the only person who gets my need for solitude. In the bathroom I repeat to myself that it's going to be a great day. I need it to be.

I lace up my yellow tennis shoes and walk down the dark hallway that has a faint light peeking through from the kitchen. I've already heard the word Prom four times from Lauren.

"Well, well, well, look who came out of their bat cave," Ben says. I try to catch my breath.

After looking at them from the hallway for three seconds, I finally say, "Hey, guys, I'm happy you're here. Don't get mad, but I haven't thought anything about my dress today. I didn't even think we'd see each other for a while. I'd also like to get some coffee. I'm barely awake."

Sarah comes over and gives me a hug. Her long red hair looks like a princess and her green eyes are full of so much love. "We came here early, I hope that's okay, Lucy. I do agree with Ben. You should get out of the house. Too many bad memories here I bet. Also, anything is better than school. Being a senior's worthless."

I laugh, "Are you serious? It's like hell. And Lauren seems excited enough for the both of us."

Lauren says, "I can hear you! Of course I'm excited! It's going to be so awesome. Luis is even getting excited now! I already have a few colors I think would be perfect for you. I just can't believe prom week's starting tomorrow. It's going to be the best night of our lives! I love you, girls. Now, let's get that coffee Lucy was talking about!"

Ben looks at her. "Not to be rude or anything, but you already sound like you've drunk a bunch of coffee this morning. Can I borrow some of your energy?"

Lauren gasps. "This is all-natural happiness, Ben. I'm just so happy about everything and that Lucy wants to go now. I'm also wide awake because Luis picked out his own tie this morning! I can't believe he took the extra initiative. Best boyfriend ever!"

Sarah chimes in, "Wow, thanks Luis. Making me look bad. I haven't even decided what color I want yet."

I interrupt the pity party that's about to start. I can feel it brewing like a witch's potion. "Hey, Sarah, did you figure out who your date's going to be? I know you couldn't decide at the diner."

"Yes, I actually did! I'm going with Elizabeth from my history class. I told you about her. Well, mostly that she's cute. But, we were texting this morning and she actually asked me!"

Tiffany gives her a high five. "That's amazing! I was right. Waiting for the bathroom together makes the world of a difference. Also, girls are way better. Sorry, Ben."

I say, "Enough small talk. Let's get this started. I'm just ready to find my dress and be done with today."

Lauren responds, out of breath again, "Oh, my goodness. Thank you, Lucy, for saying something. I was about to burst. Prom shopping it is!"

Sarah rolls her eyes. "If she says prom again, I'm going to strangle her. I don't know how much I'm going to last today, Luce. I'm going a little crazy. At least you're here."

I whisper, "Dude, same. Let's get this over with. I'm ready to go back to bed."

I kiss Ben goodbye. "Text me if you need anything. Text me lots of pictures of Snowball. Don't miss me too much. Are there any colors for your dress shirt you want me to avoid?"

Ben puts his hand on his chin. "Hmm, I don't want bright pink. Everything else is free game because we all know I look amazing in anything."

"Wow, you're such a weirdo," Lauren says.

"Yes, he's a weirdo. But he's all mine."

"I hope Elizabeth and I are just as cute together. I'm not having second thoughts, but I'm worried about our level of cuteness," Sarah says. I roll my eyes. What a bizarre thing to worry about.

I give Snowball a hug, Ben a kiss, find my green purse, and head for Lauren's sea-turtle-adorned car. Maria and Tiffany quickly follow. Lauren drives us forty-five minutes to the closest mall. Tiffany and Maria are close behind. I'm grateful to be going somewhere air-conditioned that has clothes I'd want to wear outside of town.

The usual places to get clothes in a rush are the two thrift stores in town. The thrift stores are called Tango and Mango. No joke. The stores seem to be stuck in the eighties since everything's always neon colored. I'm not joking. The clothes usually have the smell of old people, reminding me of those homes people put their grandparents in. They also always have missing zippers or extra buttons somehow. I'm glad we're going somewhere that's clean and serves soft pretzels.

Before I get lost in dresses today, I text Ben: Will you be there for Chuck today if he needs it? I feel bad for not saying bye or anything.

He texts back: Chuck just woke up and I told him you went shopping. He made a cup of coffee and went back to bed. Now, go enjoy your friends!

I laugh and feel better. I'm glad Chuck isn't expecting things from me today. I have nothing to give.

We enter through the automatic doors and the air-conditioning hits me. It's perfect. The cool air feels so nice. My skin's way too used to the desert heat that I get goosebumps. I see women who look like they spent three hours getting ready with pink lipstick caked on multiple layers of orange faces. A little girl carrying a red balloon throwing a tantrum because her parents won't give her a quarter to get a gumball. Men carry their partner's purses, looking like they're ready to go home, just like me. It smells like sadness and for some reason cinnamon in here. I already regret coming.

CHAPTER TEN

"Okay, Lucy," Lauren's saying. "Where would you like to go first?"

I sigh. But I don't ask, *Am I allowed to say home?* All I can think about is Ben, Snowball, and watching movies. I never get what I want. "You won't like my answer. But I won't be a downer. I guess let's find the store with the prettiest dresses."

She finds a store called Sparkle Swamp. Sparkle Swamp is true to its name. Everything here is either full of fake gemstones or glitter. Some lace is fine, but being covered in glitter sounds completely awful. I'm pretty sure the glitter would stick everywhere and the material would be scratchy. I'm all about smooth, loose, and comfy clothing. If I could wear silk robes all day, I totally would.

It looks like most of the dresses here are also pink, a color I despise the most. Growing up, my mom used to dress me in everything pink. She told me that even when I was born, she put a pink bow in her bag and brought it to the hospital. After the doctors washed me off, it went immediately in my hair. I don't even think babies have enough hair to support a bow, but I guess I did. Looking at the color now still brings back memories of bad times I try to forget. I keep having thoughts of that disgusting, ugly color. Maybe if I try the visual exercise, I'll feel better.

I see myself in a pink dress with white tights that always bunched up at the ankles, waiting to go to church while my mom gets ready.

I see the tubes of pink lipstick lining the bathroom counter in rows matched by shade. My mom had too much makeup and hair products, so she took over the guest bathroom. She'd put this hideous salmon-colored lipstick on both of us for special occasions, like Christmas and Easter.

I see her pink blush container shaped as a seashell. She always did layers of pink blush in winter months so she didn't look so pale. In the part of Arizona where I live, it tends to snow a lot during December. My mom didn't like anyone knowing she lost her tan, including herself.

When we moved in with Chuck, I got my own room. I was so excited and she told me we'd paint it together any color I wanted. I wanted teal blue because I always dream about the ocean or yellow for the color of giraffes—my favorite animal. Instead, I got salmon pink. I didn't tell her until a few years ago that I hated it because I didn't want her to get mad.

Sarah's voice enters my thoughts. "LL? Lucy? Why are you not responding to me? Are you with us?"

I come out of my haze of pink. Thank goodness. "Yeah, I'm here."

Maria puts her arms around my shoulders. "Well, honey, I've noticed sometimes you get this blank look on your face, and you don't respond to people. Do you just think a lot, or are you ignoring us?"

Lauren says, "Don't ignore us, Lucy. We love you so much. Today's such an important day. Dresses are always fun to try on. You're going to look great. I think if we do your hair right and get you the right makeup, you could even look like a princess."

Tiffany steps in. "Let's not overwhelm her. If she's not feeling great, she's justified. If you haven't noticed, there's a lot going on. Besides, Maria, you know Dad used to do the same thing of zoning out. He used to say his thoughts consumed him, and he was trying to center himself. Sometimes, even for me, being in the moment is the hardest thing in the world."

I roll my eyes. "So, I looked at the pink dresses and started to not feel very good. I just hate that color. It reminds me— I can't describe it. I just get sad when I see pink or anything with pink on it. I refuse to buy anything that color. So yeah. Sorry, everyone." I don't go into detail about how much it affects me. I don't want to go into the sadness I feel even looking at it. I feel like I've burdened them enough.

"Want me to call Ben?" Lauren says. Talking to Ben is a great idea. She hands me her rose-gold phone, of course, and after two rings, he answers.

"Hello?" he says in his tired voice. "What's going on?"

Laughing, I say, "It's me, Lucy. I'm kind of having a breakdown at the store. Everything's pink here."

Ben yawns. "Well, just don't buy a pink dress and leave that store. I know you hate the color, and I refuse to wear it too. So just go to a new store and try on blues and greens. You look best in those colors anyway, and I look good in anything, as you know. So don't worry about me. I love you."

He always knows exactly what to say. In the background, I hear Snowball meowing. "Aw, I hear Snowball!"

"Of course. She came to the phone as soon as she heard you. She misses her kitty momma. I'm going back to sleep, Luce, but stay strong, and I'll see you soon."

I hang up and tell the four ladies, "I'd like to go to another store that's not called Sparkle Swamp."

Lauren, who's the leader of the pack, smiles. "Yes, of course. Let's go!"

We pass Teenage City, one of my least favorite stores. The store window is full of mannequins in donut leggings, glitter crop tops, and unicorn slippers. I want some of those slippers, but we're here for a dress. I need to focus.

Maria spots Williamstons. "Look! There's a wedding dress in the window!"

"Babe, this day is for the girls. Not our wedding," Tiffany says.

"Sorry. You're right. Want to go look, Lucy?"

"Yes, good plan. I agree with Maria. Is everyone okay with this plan?"

Sarah and Lauren give a thumbs-up. I immediately see dresses that aren't pink or sparkly. Score! I look in the plus-size section since I don't want to have to squeeze into tiny dresses. As I said before, I prefer being comfy rather than tight all the time. This is going way better than I thought. Take that pink and glitter. You don't win this time!

Tiffany comes up to me. "Hey, I just wanted to say I'm sorry for everything you were feeling earlier. Thinking about the past isn't always easy and having my sister as your mom couldn't have been easy either. Anything you need from me?"

"Maybe a time machine so today can go a lot faster."

"Oops. I threw it away a while ago."

Sarah drags me away from her. "Lucy, you need to try some stuff on. Lauren's getting upset."

I hate trying on clothes. I always think of the times when I'd put stuff on, and my mom would always say things like *That would be cuter if you fit in it. You need to lose some weight." Or "Don't embarrass me, Lucy. Try something else."* After a while, I decided I didn't want to go shopping with her anymore. It worked out nicely because she just dropped me off at the mall, went to the bars, and came back a while later to get her own clothes. I think she had an unspoken rule that she had to get clothes too, whenever I did. Come to think of it, every birthday I've ever had she got herself a birthing present as a reminder of what she called *the pain she had to endure for me to be alive.* Who does that?

I browse around and put a yellow dress, a red strapless, an eggplant purple one, and two dark blue ones on my arm. I head to the awful dressing rooms.

I look at my body in just my bra and underwear and think I look like a double-breasted pear. My boobs take up more than half my body weight and my stomach protrudes like a filled-up balloon. I just wish I could shave them off. I'd fit in my clothes better.

Lauren knocks on the dressing room door. "Lucy, are you okay? Did you die in there?"

I put on the closest dress I can see. It's yellow like a beautiful sunflower. It has two thick shoulder straps. It's such a nice fit.

I open the door. "Will you zip this for me?"

I hear the zipper go all the way up from my lower back to my shoulders. It fits. I turn around and face the mirror. I look good. Is this what it feels like to be pretty?

I see Maria in my reflection. "You look beautiful. Yellow looks nice with your eyes. I love it."

I twirl around. It's perfect for dancing too. Ever since I was a child, I've loved dancing. I used to spin around like a ballerina every chance I had. I'm not saying I'm good at it, though.

"What do you think, Sarah and Lauren?"

"Oh my god, Lucy. That's perfect! You look incredible. Are you sure you don't want to try anything else on?" Lauren says.

"Sure, I'll try on one more. Just one." I shut the door and try on the dark-blue one with velvet sleeves. I put it over my head, but it doesn't want to go over my boobs. Lame.

"Any luck?" Lauren says.

"Yeah, no. This one's is too small. I'm just getting the yellow one." I get dressed quickly and am ready to leave the store.

Lauren says, "Didn't you have a red and purple one, too? I remember you bringing them in with you or am I just imagining things?"

How does she do that? That's amazing.

"No, you're not imagining things. But, how do you even remember that? You saw me holding them for less than a minute!"

"I don't know how I remember it, but I'm glad I'm not going crazy. Well, too crazy."

I pretend to try the red and purple ones on. I am okay with my body right now, but I know that feeling can be taken away fast. I need to protect myself at all costs right now. I'm honestly feeling like I'm on a seesaw where one side I'm left in complete despair and not going to Prom at all. The other side is my state of mind right now, happy with my body and ready to enjoy my future. Even if parts of it are going to be hard.

"I'm so jealous of the yellow dress you found. It curves to your body perfectly and it's the first dress you tried on." Sarah gives my elbow a shove, "You're a bitch," she says with a wink.

I say, "I'm not a bitch! Trust me when I say I would've become one if I had to try on more dresses. not feeling that today or ever. I have to get a dress shirt and tie for Ben, though."

Walking through the men's department of this oversized store, I can't help but think of how fortunate the people who wear typical men's clothes are. I see the ties with paisley prints, polka dots, and even the occasional palm tree. The fresh snow-white dress shirts line the walls on perfectly lined-up hangers. They almost look like domino pieces. One goes out of place and they'd certainly all fall. My favorite dress shirts so far are the oranges and the purple ones that look like grape bubblegum. Should we match? They look so comfortable and easy to put on.

While running my hands over the various silver and gold cufflinks, I hear Tiffany talking to Maria. "Babe, it's going to be so hard deciding what outfit I want to marry you in. I want to have at least six weddings to make sure all my outfit ideas can be seen by everyone. We'll have to come back when Lucy's done. I love everything here."

Maria, who has her hand on her hip, sighs. "How about this? We get divorced and then get married again. That way we could have another wedding!"

Lauren runs over to me with a few shirts in her hands. "Lucy, did you find a shirt for Ben? I found a few to help you. I'm glad you two are going to wear yellow! It's such a happy color! Luis and I are wearing purple. I think purple will be perfect with my red hair. I wouldn't want us to completely match. That sounds like kids in matching outfits with their parents on Christmas cards or something."

As annoying as Lauren's been, she does care. She's also the closest thing I have to a sister besides Sarah. She wants the best for me even if it's something as small as a shirt choice

I find a yellow long-sleeve shirt and a white tie with T-Rexes on it for Ben and go to one of the cashiers to pay. Lauren, Sarah, and Maria are looking at handbags. I have one already so I don't need to spend money on another. I have the money my grandpa gave me, so paying for everything won't be a problem. Thank goodness.

Tiffany chases after me. "Lucy, wait up!"

I wonder what she needs. "Okay, what's going on?"

Out of breath, she says, "Maria and I want to pay for your and Ben's things. It's the least we can do. This is your last night of fun with your friends for a while."

I want to say no, but the money's tempting to keep. It feels like money's not a problem for them, or even a worry. I'm going to go for it.

"Thank you so much. I appreciate it. Grandpa gave me some money, but I wanted to keep that for Seattle. Did you secretly put the envelope in my room?"

She hugs me with tears in her eyes. "Yes, I did. His dying wish was to have us be a family again. Oh, Lucy, I wish you could've met him. He loved you so much. He was my favorite person in the world. You must promise me this year at Christmas we'll all be together. His blue eyes shined brighter than the lights every year. His birthday was on December twenty-second and to make it extra special for him, I'd celebrate the two separately."

"How did he love me? He didn't even know me…"

"He did know you, though. He sent your mom money every month to make sure that you always had enough food and school supplies."

"Serious? My mom was always talking bad— said he was the worst. Why would she lie about that?"

Tiffany puts her head in her hand in disgust. "I don't know why Kelly did a lot of the things she did, Lucy. But, let's not drive ourselves crazy trying to figure that out. We have to be okay with not knowing. You understand?"

I nod my head because I get it. I've tried my entire life to figure out my mom. Why does she drink so much? Why is it so hard for her to wear clothes that aren't meant for 16-year olds and most recently, why did she kill Raymond?

A part of me knows I have to just accept it. I'm her kid; not a therapist or some other kind of mental health professional. I decide to change the subject and make it something positive. Like the grandpa I wish I could've known. The one whose bloodline swims in my veins. The one whose memories will live on and bring joy to those who loved him.

"Well, remember after this, we 're having the memorial. I may have never met him, but he definitely sounds amazing."

"He was amazing just like you, Lucy."

Everything Mom ever told me about him was a lie. It sucks learning the truth with Mom not here. Aside from him setting boundaries with mom, I can't help wonder what he smelled like or if he liked to paint as much as me.

My phone rings. It's Ben. "Lucy, you need to come home right away!" Ben says, his voice full of absolute horror.

Did someone else die? "What's going on, Ben? Is Snowball okay?"

"We're fine. Mick Kane called earlier looking for you. He said we need to come down to the police station right away. It's something about your mom. He wouldn't give me any other details, but he sounded serious. "When can you be home? Did you find a dress at least?"

Is something wrong with my mom? I feel the color drain from my face and my brain pulses. My brain feels like an orange that someone is trying to squeeze all the juice out of. The tingles move all the way down to my feet.

Somehow, I manage to respond, "Yes, I got a dress. I got a shirt and tie for you, too. Will you go with me to the police station, please? I don't want to go by myself. Is Chuck going to come with us? I bet he wants to know what's going on, too."

"Yeah, he'll probably come with us. He just woke up, he's taking a shower. He said something about getting powdered sugar donuts and chocolate milk before you get home. He mumbled that it's not Sunday yet he's still going to get them. I had no idea what he was talking about."

I smile because despite mom fucking things up again without even being here, Chuck is still trying to protect me. I feel lucky despite my breakdown brewing.

"Sounds good. I'll see you soon. Love you." I say and hang up.

Everyone's crowded around the small register area. I feel boxed in and like my skin is crawling. I wish Ben were here. He's always calmer and more collected than me. "Lucy, are you all right?" Sarah asks.

Tiffany and Maria look worried. They search my eyes, but I don't want to make eye contact because I think I'd start crying. "No, not. My life just feels like a hurricane trying to swallow me whole. The annoying thing is that it's winning right now."

Within a millisecond, I do start crying. Hurricane Lucy is in full swing. The tears don't want to stop. Why do I always cry in the most embarrassing spots? Everyone must think I'm crazier than I feel. I cried in the diner yesterday and now here in the middle of the store.

They all crowd around me and give me a huge group hug.

I struggle for air and pull away; my lungs can't take it... "I need to go home. Ben got a call from the detective on my mom's case, Mick Kane. Mick's great, but he's the last person I wanted to talk to right now. I'm pretty sure there's something going on with my mom."

Tiffany says, "Lucy, I'm so sorry to see you upset. We paid for your dress, and Ben's stuff as well. Let's get out of here."

With tense shoulders and a stern jaw, I respond, "Thank you. I appreciate that more than you know. I'm ready for whatever it is. I'm glad I have you all here for me. I wouldn't have made it this far without all of you."

They all smile at me and I know that I have a family. A family outside of mom.

We head to the parking garage. The air smells like rotten garbage and spoiled eggs. The heat makes the disgusting smells stick to my skin, it creates beads of sweat on my forehead. I struggle to keep one foot in front of the other without feeling like I'm going to fall. All this crying has made me lightheaded.

I say, "Lauren and Sarah, I'll talk to you later. Thanks for everything today. Love you, guys."

"We love you too. See you soon," Lauren and Sarah say.

I get in the convertible with Maria and Tiffany. They blast Limp Heart's first album, Lightning Dreams, which is my favorite, while we drive through the dry heat. As the lead singer, Madi Sample, carries her tune, the cacti lining the roads reminds me I'm still stuck here. Heartbroken about my mom and missing her more and more as the days go on. I don't know how much bad news I can take. I wonder what kind of trouble she's in.

Tiffany looks in the rear-view mirror. "You all right, kid?"

"I think so. I'm just worried about my mom, mostly. Also, I feel bad we didn't get to do the memorial for grandpa yet. Can we do it soon?"

"Yes, of course. We can do it whenever. I'm not worried."

I'm doing the color exercise to become more present. All I can think about is being in that jail cell with her. It's not a happy place to be. I don't know what I'd do if I couldn't watch movies and I doubt they have vegetarian meals.

I see Maria's purple hair slicked back in a ponytail.

I see my yellow dress. It's super beautiful. I can't believe I'm about to say this, but prom's going to be fun. A distraction sounds ideal right now.

I see my yellow tennis shoes with white shoelaces.

"Lucy, do you want to stop and get some food somewhere? I'm sure you're hungry," Tiffany says.

"I'm definitely starving. But, I think we could go after we go to the police station," I respond while Rick Sample sings about love.

"So, Lucy, I want to hear about your childhood," Maria says.

"Well, it was like everyone else's, I guess. It was shitty sometimes, but that's normal."

Tiffany giggles. "To say you had a shitty life is quite the understatement, my dear niece. I think anyone would lose their mind or become addicted to drugs with a mom like yours."

"It's honestly okay. I never went hungry or anything."

"True, but it doesn't mean that you didn't struggle. Assholes are assholes." Tiffany says while her voice becomes like my therapist's. Soothing yet concerned.

Maria says, "Lucy, we're here for you know. Okay?"

I grab her hand and say, "Thank you."

We finally pull into the driveway. I don't understand why everyone thinks my stories are always sad. It's not like I'm homeless or on the streets. We always had enough to wear and I always had warm showers, except for the few times when Mom forgot to pay the water bill. It may have been all grandpa's money, but it wasn't all bad.

I take the white bag with my dress in it, Ben's shirt, and the amazing T-Rex tie and run through the front door to Ben. He and Snowball fell asleep while eating popcorn and watching some movie with lots of fake blood. We recently discovered how much Snowball likes popcorn. It's cute. I love hearing her crunch.

She wakes up, her little green eyes opening. She jumps off the couch and circles my legs while looking up at me meowing.

CHAPTER ELEVEN

While she's circling, Ben wakes up. I think her purrs and meows broke him out of his dreams. Glad it wasn't me.

He gets up from the couch and gives me a huge hug.

In a scratchy voice, he tells, "Lucy, my love, So happy you're home. Missed you. I'm sorry for cutting the shopping trip short."

"It's okay. I found a dress."

Maria and Tiffany say, "Hi Ben!"

I unzip the white bag and show him the yellow beauty. I think he likes it.

He beams, "Lucy Love, it's perfect."

Not so fast there, Mr. Davis. I'm not done yet. I still have stuff for you, too."

I pull out the tie and dress shirt. His eyes twinkle like a Christmas tree. "Oh, my goodness, you didn't. Are these T-Rexes?"

He pulls me close and kisses me. The kiss is filled with so much passion, I swear I see fireworks like they do in those dumb, cheesy movies.

I radiate like a shooting star and grab his hand. "I'm glad you like them. I wanted to find a happy medium for us both."

"You did perfect, Lucy."

Tiffany gives us both a hug. "You two are super cute. I'm glad you feel better, Lucy. Ben, you're the best. Thanks for calming her down and letting her know Mick Kane called."

Just hearing *Mick Kane,* is enough to send me into a spiral again. He holds the key to what's going on with Mom more than anyone. Now I do want to get this done, I need sleep and to know what to do at court for my mom soon.

It's hard but I say, "Well, I'd like to go to the station as soon as possible. I'm so exhausted and starving. Did Mick send you the address?"

"He said just to meet him at the police station downtown Should Maria and Tiffany come?" He looks at them.

Tiffany boasts, "I'd like to be there for Lucy as much as possible. I honestly don't care too much about Kelly now."

Maria nods. "Yes, I agree."

I ask, "Is Chuck here?" Right as he walks out of his room

"Hey kiddo. Are we all going to go together?"

"I was thinking we should. Get this over with. I need to find out if it's even necessary to get her a lawyer or not."

"Let me figure out the lawyer thing, Lucy." Chuck grins. "Hey, there's some chocolate milk in the fridge. And some donuts on the counter for you."

Despite my wanting to get down to the station sooner, I know that I need those donuts and milk. Difficult times like this sometimes require comfort.

With my mouth full, I ask, "Anyone want one?"

Ben laughs, "Oh, Lucy. You look so cute, but no I don't."

No one else does either, so I'm just left enjoying the sugar on my own. Fine by me. I didn't want to share anyway.

We head to the red convertible that has become almost silhouetted by the bright sunset. The sky has changed from blue to a deep orange sherbet fading into cotton candy pink. Life can be great sometimes even if I forget that 98% of the time.

We enter the silver double doors of the police station and Mick Kane's in plain sight, sitting at his desk. He's distracted by a thick file of paperwork and his left hand is on his head. He looks tired. I see bags forming under his eyes.

Mick notices us and stands. He walks over and puts his huge, wrinkled hand out. "Hey, Lucy. Ben. I'm glad you're here. How are you?"

"We're fine. Now, let us have it. We can't keep wondering if she's dead or not." Chuck says

Mick says, "Oh, Chuck! Didn't even see you there. Let's get this done."

He looks at Tiffany and Maria. "I'm sorry I don't remember your names. Have we met before?"

Tiffany shakes his hand. "Hi, I'm Tiffany, Lucy's aunt, and Kelly's sister. This is Maria, my fiancé. No, we haven't met."

Mick chuckles to himself. "I still can't believe Kelly has a sister. The way she acts, I thought she was an only child."

Is Mick even allowed to say stuff like that? Probably not, but I guess he's just comfortable with us.

Tiffany crosses her arms and looks defensive. Her eyes are black as she looks at Mick.

"What's that supposed to mean? Do you have a problem with my sister? Aren't you supposed to be a professional or something?"

What the fuck is Tiffany doing? She hasn't defended my mom once since she's been here. I don't understand what's going on.

Maria nudges Tiffany. "Babe, calm down. He's just doing his job. I'm sure he's not being mean on purpose."

Mick responds and his voice changes to a strong detective again— stern and direct. "Well, I apologize for that. I'm glad you guys came down. We have a lot to talk about. Let's get some chairs."

His desk only has two which means some of us are going to have to stand. His desk is also extremely open to the public and I bet everyone can hear everything we're about to talk about. I don't like that at all. I feel like throwing up with the anxiety. I hope she's not dead, too. I can't deal with the idea of two dead bodies in less than a month.

I see Ben's orange hair and perfect curls like always.

I see my chipped white fingernails.

I see the blue uniforms on the police officers who keep walking by us. It almost feels like they're trying to hear our conversation to know what's going on. I wonder if Mick told them anything. About my mom. I mean, I'm sure they know some things, but I hope they don't know *everything*.

"I don't trust any of you pigs and I don't want my sister's business floating around here."

Mick gets angry. "Listen here, Tiffany, I'm not one of those pigs you're speaking of. I'm a detective and am doing everything I can to keep Lucy safe."

Tiffany gulps, we all hear it. Her face is a nice shade of strawberry now. "I'm sorry, Mr. Kane. No one wants to hear that their sister is in prison ya know? I'm just annoyed."

Mick whispers, "Yes, I know. I became a detective because I told myself I'd never let anyone rot behind bars for crimes they didn't commit. My dad spent my entire life in prison for a crime he didn't commit. I talked to him once a week when I was a child, but he always forgot my birthdays. Holidays were the hardest. Last year, he died in the same prison cell he spent forty years in. If you could refrain from calling me a pig, I'd appreciate it."

I had no idea about Mick's past. Chills run down my arms and tears well-up in my eyes. Am I crying again?

With a nose full of snot and tears dripping down my face, I hug Mick. "I had no idea you went through that. I'm so sorry. Does it get easier having a parent in prison? I can't even think about it yet. I don't know what I'm going to do, especially on Christmas. "Did you have a mom?"

Mick hugs me back and I swear he has tears in his eyes as well. "Well, Lucy, I must say, it doesn't get easier. But we find better ways to deal with it. You seem to have a good support system. My mom became addicted to meth when my dad was taken from us. She's been sober for five years now. She's old and lives in a retirement home. She's starting to forget who I am. It sucks, but that's life I guess."

I feel grateful that Mick is sharing all of this with us. I know it's probably against police protocol completely, but I don't care. It helps me get to know him and feel less alone.

"Can we go somewhere more private?" Chuck says.

"Yes, of course." Mick says, fighting back his tears. He clears his throat and looks back to normal.

The lights are dim in this hallway. As Ben and Mick lead the way, their clothes seem to almost glow among the bare white walls. Ben looks tiny compared to Mick. We go into the interrogation room. Mick faces us on one side of the table. I'm about to hang onto every word this man says. "So, Lucy, are you ready to answer a bunch of questions?"

I think about it for a second. "Yes, I'm ready. I just need to make sure—"

Tiffany interrupts, "We're here for you, Lucy. You got this."

Maria says, "Yes, Lucy, we're here. Breathe."

I'm filled with fear as Mick opens his mouth. "Your mom said you played a big part in helping her murder Raymond. Is this true?"

Did I hear him right? My mom's accusing me of helping her murder Raymond. What the fuck? "Wait, what? Can you repeat that?"

"Your mom's saying you were a big part of murdering Raymond. Is this true or not? This is serious business, Lucy."

Ben gets up and hits his chair so hard it falls to the ground. "What the fuck? You're joking, right? Lucy could never kill someone. Kelly's the worst person I've ever met for blaming her only kid for murder. You can't believe her, right?"

Maria says, "Mick, there's no way it could be Lucy."

"Everyone, shut up!" I scream. "Please. I didn't kill Raymond. I just want to get out of Arizona as soon as I graduate. Why would I choose to spend more time here than I need to? I hate it here."

Chuck says, "I was home the night of the murder. Lucy didn't leave her room all night. Her music was so loud!"

Mick says, "Listen, Lucy, I'm not saying you're guilty. But, I need to record you having a credible alibi. Officially this time."

"But, I showed you those texts to Ben. Isn't that enough?"

"No, it's not. We need to figure this out before you go to jail, too. You need a stronger alibi."

"Okay, I'd like to do that now. I'm so pissed. How could she do this to me?"

My heart races. My hands sweat. I feel like an elephant is sitting on top of my chest. My air supply seems limited now. Everything's morphing into one like at the diner.

I wake up and everyone's standing around me. Ben pushes my hair out of my face.

I sit up. "Can I have some water? What happened?"

"Lucy, you passed out again." Ben says.

Mick says, "You passed out. We were talking about your mom accusing you of helping her kill Raymond Williams and then just plop on the ground you went. It was like that day in the store."

My mom's the worst. She's hurt me in the past many times, but it has never felt like this. Betrayal. I want her to feel this pain like me, so she knows how it feels to have your heart ripped out. I can't believe she had the audacity to call and ask for gummy worms. She isn't getting anything from me.

Never again.

I sit in my chair in the interrogation room. I have no connection to my brain and mouth. I'm too angry to speak. My chest and head throbs. A nap for a few weeks sounds great. That way, my wish to be out of Arizona will come true. Out of Arizona and finally in beautiful Seattle.

Mick crosses his hands on the desk. "Okay, Lucy, are you ready for that alibi? I can start the tape recorder whenever you're ready."

Alibi. More like I just want to go home and cry. "Listen, dude, I can't focus. I'm too upset to even form words. Can we postpone this? Like until next week?"

Mick gets up from his chair and looks me deep in the eyes. "Lucy, you aren't allowed to leave. If you leave this building without a written statement defending yourself, I'll have to assume the worst."

"Okay. I'm going to the bathroom. I'll be back to talk to you as soon as possible. Thanks."

I run to the bathroom. It needs to be unlocked by Mick and he stands right behind me.

He jingles his keys and says, "I have to stay outside while you're in here. It's protocol to ensure you don't go anywhere."

He unlocks the door. The bathroom has no mirror and the lights in here shine on me like a spotlight.

I splash some cold water on my face. It feels refreshing and wakes me up. How can I be related to someone as evil as mom? I can't believe I never listened to anyone when they told me she was so fucked up. She was supposed to be the one person I could always rely on. Don't most people have normal moms? Why can't I be normal?

A knock wakes me out of my pity party. "Lucy, are you okay in there?"

"I'll be right out." Guess I'll have my breakdown later when I'm in bed with Ben.

I walk back to the interrogation room where Ben, Chuck, Maria, and Tiffany are waiting. Ben's eyes light up as soon as I enter the room.

Mick Kane guides his hand over the table and turns on the tape recorder. "Lucy McBride, where were you on Saturday, May 9th, 2019, at 10:15 PM?"

"Well, judging by how I have no social life, I was at home. Can social media posts work as proof, Mick?"

"Yes, but they'll need to be checked by my IT guy, Al. He'll work his magic and determine if the posts were made at the place you say they were."

I open my social media app on my phone and scroll through, looking at my random photos. I have a selfie of Snowball and me that day. I put my phone on the table and show him the adorable picture.

"Here's me and Snowball hanging out that night. I remember I worked that day and Chuck said I could go home early. He was going to close everything without me. I thought it was great I got to go home before I expected. Saturday's usually my binge-watching movie day."

Mick asks, "Can I have your phone to get this date and time checked out?"

I nod and hand him my orange phone.

A random dude with long, black hair and a tan trench coat comes in. The trench coat seems so stereotypical that I can't help but laugh.

"Lucy, no laughing. This is a serious matter." Chuck whispers.

"I'm just laughing at the dude's coat. It was a good distraction."

Chuck smiles, "Yeah, I noticed that, too. We'll talk about it after. Time to be serious."

"You're right." I say while making my lips straight and appear serious.

The man in the trench coat comes back and says, "Okay, everything checks out."

"Thank you. Let's keep going. The night of the murder, was there anyone else in the store who helped Chuck close?"

"Come to think of it, no. Chuck said he would close by himself that night. We didn't have many customers, so I didn't think anything of it. Everyone usually helps with closing, but it being especially slow, I didn't think anything of it. He also said he was going to take my mom on a date later. His idea of a date is normally buying her a drink. He had a bouquet of flowers made by the store florist. It was sweet."

"That makes sense, Lucy. Your story checks out. But, that leaves us with you then, Chuck. Did you murder your dad?"

Chuck slams his fist on the table, "No! I didn't murder my dad. I didn't like him very much, but that doesn't mean I killed him. I can show you the inside of my safe. Kelly took the gun out of there. You'll see that I'm not lying."

Mick says, "Fine. We'll go through your safe. Listen now, though. I'm not allowed to do this, so this stays between all of us. Okay?"

Chuck says, "Okay. But, I'm getting tired of this. Kelly's the crazy one. Not Lucy or me."

"It doesn't matter if she's crazy or not, we still have to weigh out all of our options."

I say, "Well, then, let's head over to the house. We need to figure this out."

Tiffany and Maria walk to the front of the red convertible while Ben, Chuck, and I slide into the back seat. Sitting in the middle makes me feel shielded from any outsider or negative force.

Mick is right behind us when we arrive at the house. I take my keys out of my purse and hear crickets in their little world. I wish I was one of them. I'm sure none of them blame their kids for murdering other crickets. Being a human sucks sometimes. Well, actually, no. All the time.

"Lucy, the three of us are just going to stay here in the living room and watch TV. Is that okay?" Ben says.

"Yes, that's perfect. Thank you."

Chuck leads the way to his and mom's room. We all go straight to the overflowing closet. The closet is full of shoes—mainly heels, scarves, dresses, and lots of jackets. After some digging, the safe appears. The black box protected by the combination lock feels almost as if it's mocking me with its secrets. Chuck punches in one-nine-eight-zero on the circular number pad and the safe clicks open.

At first glance, I notice lots of blood splattered everywhere coating the inside of the tiny walls. Mick puts some gloves on.

We all notice a baby blue dress my mom always wore. It's covered in dried blood.

Mick says while holding the dress, "Well, that was easy…"

"A little too easy, it seems." I say.

"Well, let's see what else we can find, Lucy." Chuck says. Mick puts the dress in a clear plastic evidence bag. Chuck pulls out a black mask. "A ski mask? Why would this be in here?"

"I know that mask! It's the same one the killer wore according to the security cameras at the store. Kelly must've just wanted to get caught."

"Why would she want to get caught? That sounds like the worst murderer ever." I say.

"That's a mystery to me, Lucy. It's the same with some serial killers. There's this one who was named Paul Michael Stephani in the 90's who admitted his crimes anonymously to the police."

"Wow, I don't know what else to say. That's weird. But, you're welcome for her making it easy?"

Mick chuckles. "Okay, that was funny, but we need to finish looking through this. I need concrete evidence and enough fingerprints for my people to scan."

"Anything else in there, dude?"

"Yeah, just one more thing. Promise you won't freak out..."

"Yes, I won't freak out. I promise."

Chuck pulls out a black gun. "Back away and calm down. It's not going to hurt you."

Mick nods, "Lucy, you're safe. The gun has no way of firing or hurting anyone. I found all the evidence I need and your alibi checks out."

Still panicked about the gun, I tremble while my voice shakes. "So, what does this mean? Are we done for the night?"

"Yes, we are all done. I'll call you both later this week."

I walk into the living room where Ben, Maria, and Tiffany have their eyes glued to the tv.

Ben pauses the show and says, "You guys get everything figured out?"

"Yep, my mom made it easy for Mick to find out it was her. She definitely didn't plan ahead at all."

Mick says, "Yeah, it was pretty easy. Anyway, I am going to go now. I gotta take this stuff back to the station. Talk to you later."

I follow him to the front door and say, "Thanks for everything. I appreciate it."

"You're welcome. Talk to you soon."

I walk back to the living room and Tiffany says, "How does pizza sound? Maria and I will go pick it up."

Chuck slumps in the dining room chair, "Can you get some beer, too? I'm feeling used."

Tiffany says, "You feel that because you *were* used. There's no if and buts about that. But, I'm not getting any beer. From here on out, this is a sober household. No alcohol."

Chuck huffs, "Okay, fine. You're right. Alcohol doesn't solve anything."

I could just squeeze Tiffany till her eyes pop out. I feel grateful for many things right now, but people not drinking in front of me is a big one. The smell of alcohol and being around it feels like it would completely set me off.

CHAPTER TWELVE

I wake up from my pizza hangover and roll over to check my phone. It's 9:03 a.m. on Tuesday. Shit. I know it's gonna be another day of missing school.

I rush out of bed to find Tiffany or Maria. Tiffany's passed out on the couch and Maria's asleep on the armchair.

Tiffany sits up and rubs her eyes. Her hair's tousled and sticks out in four different directions. "Hi, Lucy. What's up?"

"I just realized today's Tuesday. A school day. Will you call the attendance lady, Julie, and tell her I'll be out until tomorrow? I'm not eighteen yet, so I can't call for myself."

"Do I need to call for Ben too?"

"No, he's eighteen too and can call on his own. Speaking of which, I should wake him up before he gets in trouble." I run to my room and he's snoring. He's left drool on his pillow.

He gasps for air, "What's wrong? You look like zombies are at the door or something. Why aren't you sleeping?"

Before he says anything else, I say, "Good morning! It's Tuesday, so you need to call school and tell them you'll be out until tomorrow. Tiffany's calling for me to let them know."

"Good idea. Will you hand me my phone?" he says while sitting up.

I do and then go check in with Tiffany. She gives me a thumbs-up. "I'm going back to sleep now. Night-night."

I give her a hug. "Night-night, Auntie. Thank you."

As I enter my room, I hear Ben on the phone. "Yes, I'm sick. No, I'll be back tomorrow. See you then." He sounds annoyed, but I'm glad we both have our backs covered. The last thing we need is trouble at school.

"Was it Julie?"

"Of course. She was saying it's highly suspicious that you and I are both sick at the same time. Why does it matter so much to her anyway?" Sigh. How do I nicely tell him that I just want to go back to bed? I'm so tired.

"Lucy, are your eyes shutting mid-conversation?"

"Maybe. I mean, no. Of course not." I yawn.

"Let's go back to sleep. You're obviously super tired and not interested in anything I'm saying."

I think Ben's angry, but I have no energy to make sure he's okay. I cuddle with Snowball and hope to pass out soon.

I was right. I passed out for a while. I woke up to the sound of my phone vibrating on my wooden table. I rub my eyes and look at the screen. Unknown caller. The green answer and red ignore buttons flash like traffic lights. But before I answer, the phone stops vibrating.

Oh, well.

Wait, it's ringing again. Guess someone wants to get a hold of me. A robotic voice says, "You have a collect call from Arizona State Holding Cell in Perryville. Do you accept the charges?"

In my muffled half-asleep voice, I say, "Yeah, I guess?"

"Lucy, it's Mom!" She sounds almost drunk and so full of energy. That must be nice. I can't remember a time where I felt happy.

"Mom, why are you calling me? What's up?"

"Well, I've been asking the guards every day about my mail and still no sign of gummy worms. I was just making sure you didn't die or something. I wanted to see how my baby girl doing. How are you? How's Ben?"

"No gummy worms are coming for you there never will be. I'm fine and so is Ben. Mick Kane told me you said I helped you murder Raymond. I can't believe you said something like that." I'm glad to tell her how I feel, but confrontation always makes me nervous. It always makes me feel sick.

I put her on speaker phone and get out of bed to take my pills. Maybe my anxiety meds will make everything calm down a little. I'm tired of feeling like a pile of garbage.

Her voice amplifies. "Oh, Lucy! Don't get mad at me. I did tell Mick it was you who killed Raymond because he was always so mean to you. I wanted to make sure that we'd still go to Seattle. You're just a kid, they wouldn't send you to jail!"

"That makes no sense at all, Mom. You fucked up and can't fix this. I'm so done with your lies and blaming everyone else. This ends now."

"It doesn't have to make sense, Lucy. How dare you stand up to me! I am your mother. Do you think I like being in jail, eating the same meals all the time and not wearing makeup? I did this for you, baby girl."

"Thanks, Mom? I gotta go. Your two minutes are up." I'm glad I got out of bed to take my pills. Snowball jumps on the bathroom counter. She knocks over my teal hairbrush and clear pill reminder. With shaky hands, I pet her. She keeps nudging my hand for more strokes.

"Lucy, are you on the phone? Who are you talking to?" Ben shouts from the bed.

"I was talking to my mom. She called asking for her dumb gummy worms. Can you believe that? Can she just stop being so selfish for once? I mean, I'm not perfect—"

Before I finish my sentence, Ben runs over and gives me a hug. I hug him back and put my head on his shoulder while he comforts me. He runs his fingers through my hair and drags me back to bed.

"What do you mean she asked for gummy worms? Did you tell her Mick Kane told us she framed you?" Ben says.

"Remember last time she called? She asked me to send her candy and cigarettes, and she was wondering where they were. I told her she'll never get anything from me again. Yes, I brought up the fact that she blamed me for Raymond. She's the worst." I turn away from him. I don't want him to see how upset I am.

"Well, try not to let her ruin your day again. She doesn't deserve that."

"Yeah, you're right…" I say, while feeling my arms and chest tighten.

Ben says, "Lucy, there was something I wanted to talk to you about…" I feel myself stuck in a hole of despair and barely able to hear him. He repeats himself, "LUCY!"

I pull myself out of it and say, "Sorry, yes. What is it?"

"Well, I feel neglected. I mean I know I'm supposed to be here for you and all, but no one's asked how I'm doing. Not even once."

I look at his eyes and they seem to be welling up with tears. "I had no idea you were feeling like this. Why didn't you say anything?"

"I don't know. I didn't know how to bring it up. I just feel like no one cares about me. It's just always the Lucy show."

The Lucy show? Is he serious? This is my mom in jail. How dare he make this about him. I'm the most vulnerable I've ever been in my life. "The Lucy show? Are you serious? I'm heartbroken over this. It's not like she was *your* mom."

"You're right! She isn't *my* mom, but we both know she's darn near close. I see her more than my own. I thought you would understand that." Ben grabs his clothes and gets dressed.

"Wait, don't leave. Can't we talk about this?"

"No, there's nothing left for me to say, Lucy. I'm going home." he says while walking towards his car. I stand in front of him and hope that he changes his mind.

He doesn't.

I make my way back into the house and run into my room. I make sure to lock my door and pick up my phone. I have three missed calls from Sarah, two from Lauren, and a bunch of texts.

I dig through my contacts and click on Dr. Prince. I've gone long enough without talking to her.

She picks up on the third ring, "Hi Lucy. Thank you for calling me. I was getting worried about you. How would you like to start our session today?"

Without an inhale or exhale, I say, "Hi, Doctor Prince. It's good to hear from you, too. Can we talk?"

"Yes, of course."

"Okay, cool. A lot of stuff has been going on, but I'm okay. I mean not okay. My boyfriend and I just got into a fight. I feel like a terrible person. I'm constantly tired. I'm ready for senior year to be over and I'm just so sad."

"Lucy, please slow down. Why did you and your boyfriend get into a fight? Why are you sad?"

"Well, I don't know if you know or not, but there was a murder at the grocery store I work at about a week ago. I was— it turns out my mom is actually the murderer."

"What did you say? Your mom is the murderer? Lucy, that's a big accusation and something I need to report to the authorities. Are you sure?"

I wish I could just yell and say *of course it was her*. But, I'm not about to go to a mental hospital or something.

"Yes, it was her, Dr. Prince. The authorities already know and so does my step dad. I'm sad because I feel like everything is spiraling out of control and I can't do anything about it."

"Well, in a way, you're right. This is a huge deal and when we lose a sense of control, our minds get in survival mode. But, let's focus on what you can control. How does that sound?"

I take notice of color in my rooms and focus on my breathing. I say, "Okay, that sounds good. But, I don't think anything is going to help."

"Let's start with your breathing, Lucy. Close your eyes."

I hate this dumb hippie shit. If she tells me to light some incense and to buy some vinyl records, I'm looking for a new therapist. I wait a few seconds but she says nothing about incense or records. I give in and close my eyes.

"Okay, we're going to do something called vagus nerve breathing. Have you heard of it?" I shake my head like she can see me, but I remember that we're just in a call. No video.

"No, I haven't. What does that mean?"

"It's a type of breathing that calms your nervous system. It's been known to calm signs of anxiety and make you feel a little better. Would you like to try it?"

"Sure, I'm desperate to feel better."

"Okay, so you are going to inhale for four seconds, hold for seven, and exhale for eight. Think you can try it for three minutes with me?"

This is going to be easy. Who needs help with breathing?

We try it for two and I'm already dizzy. I was wrong. Breathing is difficult. After the three minutes is up, she tells me to open my eyes. "How did that feel, Lucy? Do you feel any better?"

A part of me wants to lie to her, so I can call Ben and get this session over with. But, there's a louder voice telling me to not lie to her. She's here to help me. "No, I honestly don't. That didn't help. Can we try for five minutes?"

She almost giggles and says, "Yes, of course."

We try the vagus breathing for again for longer this time, and I feel a sense of calm. Something I'm not used to. I also feel lightheaded.

"Wow, I feel great. Thank you so much, Dr. Prince. I'll talk to you later, okay?"

I try to rush her off the phone because I'm tired of being vulnerable. Tired of people seeing who I am. A person full of insecurities and unlovable.

"Before you leave, Lucy, I'd like you to think of another mantra. I love the one you thought of about your bipolar not defining you. But,

I'm afraid that will get old. What do you think will be helpful for you? Especially during this difficult time."

I shrug my shoulders, "I don't know. How about *I'm not an idiot?*"

"That's a unique choice. Do you feel like an idiot?"

"No, not really. But, it's the first thing I could think of."

I hear her humming. Almost as if she's in deep thought. "Well, I know that your mom has brought you some problems. Let's explore that, shall we?"

I know that I should be mad at her for keeping me on the phone longer. But, there's something about her soothing voice that is making me want to continue opening up to her and healing from all of the shit going on.

"Okay, that's a good idea. Where do we start?"

"Well, how does your mom make you feel? When you think of her, what do you think about?"

"Alcohol. My childhood. Cigarettes. The mall. I don't know."

"What about your childhood?" I feel like I'm on a talk show.

"Well, there are things I haven't accepted yet. I mean sometimes when her and I talk, I still feel like a little kid again."

"That's good, Lucy. Keep going."

"Yeah, I feel like a little kid. A little kid who's wondering what I did wrong to be left alone or not as fun as alcohol. Ya know?"

"Yes, my dear. Children of alcoholics feel like this a lot. You're not alone in that."

A part of me is glad that I'm not alone in this feeling. But, it sucks to think that others do as well. "I just want to accept what happened and move on. I'm tired of beating myself up about it."

"It's better to feel things than push them away, Lucy. Remember that you are safe here and are worthy of love."

Just then, a little voice enters my brain. I know what I want my mantra to be!

Even though I feel like a child, there's nothing wrong with me. I love and accept myself completely. I repeat it out loud and Dr. Prince says, "Perfect. Keep saying it till you believe it."

I say it at least twenty more times and feel a smile come across my face. A genuine smile this time. "How will I remember this? I mean in those dark moments, sometimes I forget everything I've worked hard for."

"Write it down then! Put it on your mirror. All over your room! Your car even. Make it your phone background. Whatever you need to do, Lucy. This is all you."

"Okay, good idea! Dr. Prince, thank you so much," I say while spotting my orange notepad. I write the saying five times and decide to stick it everywhere. I also know what I have to do.

"I need to go see Ben, though. He's probably still upset at me for everything. I don't blame him. I haven't asked how he's doing with everything. Not even once."

"Okay, Lucy. Take care of yourself. We'll talk soon." She hangs up.

I find Ben's name and click on it.

He answers it on the 3rd ring. "Hi. What do you want?"

"I want you to come back over here. I screwed up and I'm sorry. I've just been in this funk of self-sabotage and I didn't think of your feelings. Please forgive me. You're my person."

He waits a few seconds and says, "You're my person, too. That's why I'm so upset. I didn't think you'd ever become this selfish. I matter, too!"

"Yes, yes you do. Now, come on! Let's get some ice cream and just laugh for a little."

"Fine, I'll be there in a few minutes. You owe me, McBride!"

I blush and say, "I know I do. We'll get all the ice cream you want."

Even though I feel like a child, there's nothing wrong with me. I love and accept myself completely.

Even though I feel like a child, there's nothing wrong with me. I love and accept myself completely.

Ben and I are way better now. We just had to talk things out. Sometimes being in a relationship with your best friend is hard because they know everything about you. While he knows everything about me and still loves me for it is great and all; I still find myself forgetting that he has feelings, too.

Our topic of conversation is now about why mom would ever be a murderer. It's making me think, what makes people murderers?

He tickles my stomach, which is my weak spot. "Well, Lucy, I can believe it. She's not going to change. I'm glad you didn't apologize and you refused to send her stuff. That's progress. What do we do now?"

Giggling from the tickles, I tell him, "I don't know. Just keep moving forward, I guess. Let's go see if Maria and Tiffany are awake yet."

Ben kisses my forehead and squeezes my hand. "Thanks for listening. I know this all sucks, but knowing that you still care about me makes a difference."

"Still care about you? You're crazy if you thought I ever stopped!" We stick our tongues out at each other and proceed to have belly laughs.

We go into the kitchen and smell pancakes. Maria and Tiffany are blasting some Glitter Tooth, singing along, and flipping pancakes. They look so happy that I don't want to disturb them.

Maria notices us and pauses the music. "Good morning, beautiful people. How are you two this morning? I noticed there was a pancake mix, so we decided to make breakfast."

"Sounds great." Ben smiles.

I round up some plates, the syrup, and the butter from the fridge. I set the table. I'm glad they cooked something. I didn't want to go anywhere today or do anything. I didn't even want to put pants on. Actually, that's every day.

In the middle of flipping one of the pancakes, Tiffany looks at me. "Wait, something's off with you, Lucy. You seem upset."

How does she always know something's wrong? I swear she can sense everything. Is she a mind reader?

"I've been better, honestly. My mom called asking if I'd sent her anything from the outside yet. She didn't apologize for blaming me for killing Raymond either. She's the worst."

"I'm sorry, Lucy, but she probably won't ever apologize." She focuses on the food. "Let's just enjoy today. We've got pancakes and everything's going to be alright."

I dance in the kitchen until the pancake batter is gone and all the pancakes are stacked high on a yellow plate. Then we sit down at the table. With my silver fork in hand, I say, "Thank you for making breakfast. I appreciate it."

Ben, who's already digging into the food, says, "Yeah, thank you!"

Maria blushes. "You're welcome, guys. Anything for you. What are we going to do today anyway?"

"I have no idea. I wasn't even wanting to put pants on, honestly," I say around a mouthful of delicious overly syruped pancakes. I forgot my phone in my room. I should go get it. Mick Kane might call or something. I eat my breakfast and try to focus on everyone at the table. My phone can wait. "So, Maria, I have a question."

"What, Lucy?" she responds while pouring herself a glass of orange juice.

"Growing up in the Philippines, did you ever see American movies?"

"No. I grew up in a small village, so we never had money to go see movies. I was always too busy pretending to be a teacher with my dolls anyway."

"Well, well, well, I think we found out what we're doing today," Ben exclaims. His hands are clasped together with excitement. His face looks the same as when I find him a new dispenser.

At the same time, we say, "It's horror, fake blood movie watching time!"

Tiffany rolls her eyes. "I'm actually excited about this. The best part of those movies are the stupid choices the people make. I mean, who hangs out at a graveyard at night, thinking it's a good idea? Do they not think at all?"

CHAPTER THIRTEEN

Ben sticks a huge bite of pancakes in his mouth before running to the living room to find the DVDs. He's like a child on Christmas morning.

"They're in a movie, Tiffany!" I say. "Give them a break. Can you blame them? All logic goes out the window. It definitely beats a phone call that kills you if you don't answer or a stupid clown, right? I mean, who even likes clowns, they're—"

Before I can finish, Maria laughs. "Oh, Lucy, you're the cutest nerd ever. Let's watch a movie. But first, we do need to have a little bit of a memorial for Frank. We've waited way too long for this. Should we get Chuck?"

"Yeah. I know he buried Raymond without everybody, but he may want to remember his dad in his own way."

I scream for him, "Chuck! Are you there?"

He walks into the kitchen in his yellow work shirt and says, "Yeah, I'm right here. What's up?"

"What are you all dressed up for?"

"I'm opening up the store today. Just doing a test run and seeing what needs to be done. I want to be officially open again on Saturday. It's been two weeks. I'm ready to go back."

"Ready to go back? Who are you?" Chuck usually hates working.

"Very funny. I just miss my routine. Dad would've wanted the store to stay open."

"You're right. But, have a pancake before you leave." He takes one off the top and heads out the door. He didn't even put any syrup or butter on it!

"Lucy, we are getting everything ready. Come back when you're ready." Maria screams from the living room.

I go into the living room and sit on the couch. Snowball's passed out between Tiffany and me. That cat could sleep for weeks at a time. Jealous.

Maria's gone out to the convertible to get a green blanket. She puts it up to her nose and says, "Still smells like Dean. Right, Tiffany?"

Tiffany says, "Yes, you're so right! Peppermint and cigars. The best combination." Tiffany spreads the blanket on the floor with white votive candles. Ben holds a matchbox.

"Are you two ready?" I say while tears already form in my eyes. I've never had anyone close to me die before. I know I never knew him, but I feel a sense of grief. A grief for a life without someone who would have meant so much.

Tiffany has a wooden box in her hand, and she says, "Hi dad. It's me. I just wanted to say hi and that I love you. Maria and I saved your green blanket. We figured you'd want us to have it. Lucy and Ben are here, too."

"Hi grandpa. It's me, Lucy. I have heard we are a lot alike. I wish I could have met you. You seem like a pretty cool guy. Thanks for the money for Seattle. I love you."

Ben says, "Hey Dean. I hope you're doing okay wherever you are. I heard you like green. So, do I! Also, thanks for the money. Wish I could've met you, too. You would have been proud of Lucy. She's awesome. So is Tiffany. You left behind some good genes."

Maria starts crying, "Hey Dean. I miss you. We are having a lot of fun here with Lucy and Ben. She's such a good girl. I wish you could be here with us. You would've looked great in a tuxedo at Tiff's and my wedding. I miss our ice cream dates. Love you."

Maria goes into Tiffany's arms and just cries. Tiffany cries with her.

Tiffany pulls away and says, "Hey dad. Me again. I love you. How are you up there? I miss you more than you know, but I am so happy to be around Lucy and Ben. Did you see Kelly went to jail? Crazy, right?"

I step in and say, "Should we have a moment of silence for him or something?" Everyone nods their heads and we all sit in silence for a few minutes. Ben and I blow out the clear glass votive candles. Everyone is smiling and I feel a sense of relief. I still wish I could have met him, but I feel a sense of closure now.

Ben says, "Anyone up for The Phone Call from Death?"

"YES! I'd love to!" Maria says.

"Only if we make popcorn." Tiffany says with a stuffy nose from crying.

"Yes, I will for sure make popcorn. Are you doing okay?" I ask Tiffany.

She puts her thumb up and says, "Definitely."

My heart still aches, but I immediately get annoyed. Annoyed by the four walls around me. I am beginning to hate this house more and more. The black couch is falling apart. The walls are so creaky and are full of so many secrets. The bathrooms are full of so much mold that it's starting to form rings on the ceilings. I swear there are rats on the roof because every night before bed, I hear scampering feet up there. The closets are stacked full of my mom's clothes and Chuck's car parts. I hate it.

After the movie, I decide that I want to get rid of some of Mom's things. I'm getting annoyed seeing her stuff everywhere. The way my mom dresses is not anything I idolize or would wear in a million years. I'm not a fan of belly shirts, lots of pink, or glitter. Her belongings are taking up space and I'd rather the house be empty of things that remind me of her. A garage sale sounds perfect.

While Ben tries to convince Maria to watch the next horror movie, I pose an idea to the group. "Hey, guys, what do you think about having a garage sale on Sunday after prom? I don't want to keep looking at my mom's stuff."

Ben stops talking and grabs my hand. "Lucy Love, that's a perfect idea. We can add the money we make to our college funds."

Tiffany says, "I'm in. Let's get big poster boards to advertise the garage sale with the address on it. I also think they have price stickers you can buy. Does that sound good to you, guys?"

Maria puts her arm around Tiffany's shoulder and smiles. "Yep. That's a perfect idea. Just like you are to me."

Ben shakes his head. "Slow the cuteness train down, or I'm going to vomit. Let me tie my shoes and we can head to the Dollar Hut."

Maria, Tiffany, and I line up at the door like we're in elementary school, waiting for Ben to be done.

I put his hand in mine. "Let's go, my love."

As we drive down the road, I think about how awesome a time machine would be. I'd go into the future a year from now where everything is magically worked out. I'm tired of waiting around.

The car comes to a screeching halt because Tiffany misses the left turn to the Dollar Hut. That woke me up out of my haze. Maria turns around from the passenger seat. "Some directions would've been nice, little miss. Remember, we don't live here!"

"Sorry, I totally blanked."

Tiffany parks. "It's okay. I like the idea of selling everything, but are you sure you want to do this?"

"Yes, 100%. She admitted to the murder. She's obviously not coming back."

Ben says, "Well, we can't exactly prove that. Nothing in the universe is 100%."

Maria replies to Ben's comment so sarcastically, "Yeah, Lucy. Duh…"

I see the neon-green sign as an entrance that will solve all the problems of the annoying chaos that's become the house. I find a cart and enter the swinging doors. I find some sour candy for fuel, some black markers to write on the signs—I love the smell of them too—and we find some price tags to stick on the items. Ben gets some barbecue chips. Maria finds a root beer. Tiffany snags some purple energy drink with a horse on it.

"Great timing, Lucy. Ready?" Tiffany says at the drink cooler.

"Yes, I want to get started as soon as possible." I put everything on the gray conveyor belt.

I hand the cashier my almost-brown crumpled money and the four of us leave. I'm ready to get a lot of cleaning done. The movement of the car puts chills on my skin and I take it as a sign that my body's ready for a new start as well. My mental health's been in question for too long. Seattle will happen no matter what, but I may as well enjoy the last moments I have left here. I mean, the end of high school can't be all that bad. Lauren and Sarah are the greatest friends anyone could ask for. I need to remember this when I pack everything up today. This is just a new beginning.

We zoom home at a speed that's a little too fast for me. Sometimes I get car sick and today is no exception. But the dizziness and nausea are a good distraction, lately, I feel as if my head will explode like a volcano because there's so much going on in there.

I'm glad to be home. I unload the car and put the neon poster boards on the kitchen floor. The tables still covered with makeup and hair things. I don't want to move everything off it because I'm sure Lauren and Sarah will want to use it on Saturday for prom day.

"Ben, I say with a mouth full of sour candy, "are you ready for this? It's showtime."

He grabs my arm, "Ready as I'll ever be, Lucy. What room do you want to start with?"

"I think my mom's side of the closet. We'll probably get rid of everything in there. We can lay all the stuff on the bed to go through. Maybe keep the clothes on their hangers. Let me get a trash bag for donations. We'll put anything that's too weird or no one would buy it in it." I say while scrunching my face. This candy is tangier than I thought.

"Sounds good. I'll put some music on to get us pumped up." Ben turns on Cats by Candlelight on his phone.

While *"Crazy Alien Love"* plays, Tiffany knocks on the door.

"Hey, party people, what can Maria and I do? Seems like you have this taken care of."

"Can you go through the stuff in the garage? There's a bunch of holiday decorations in there. Does that sound okay?" I hope I'm not coming off as rude.

"Sounds good, LL. See you guys later." Tiffany waves bye.

"Bye, Luce and Ben. I'll miss you," Maria jokes as she fake cries and goes into the garage to help Tiffany.

While going through my mom's clothes, it's become apparent she has way too many of them. I've already found over twenty dresses. I even found four Christmas ones. Those for sure are getting donated. I don't think anyone should be wearing sweaters that say MEOWY CHRISTMAS. How embarrassing.

Ben looks through her fifty pairs of shoes and picks up some highlighter yellow heels. "Lucy, you must wear these for prom!"

I stop laying dresses on the bed. "You're joking, right? I'd never wear those."

He winks. "Of course, I'm joking. I do think you'd look cute in heels, though."

"Thank you. Not this time, though. Yellow tennis shoes it is. However, I wonder if teal or purple might be better. What do you think?"

"You'll look good in whatever."

"Thanks, Ben."

On my way to the garage I decide to price the dresses at five dollars each. That's a bundle for Seattle right there. "Hey, guys, how's it going in here?"

Maria says, "Hey, Luce! There're too many random things we don't know about. How about we work on writing signs? We can always have more than one sale."

"I agree." Tiffany adds, "Maybe Sunday can be your mom's clothes and shoes. The next one can be household products and random trinkets."

"Why do you guys always have to be right? I am definitely overexerting myself to get this all done. But having an empty closet is a great start."

I get working and soon all the dresses are priced and Ben's going through her shoes. I don't think anyone in their right mind should have as many clothes as she does.

Tiffany comes back and puts her hand on my shoulder and says sarcastically, "Do you think the prison will let us send clothes instead of cigarettes and candy?"

"Very funny. Now, let me get back to work, so we can have more time to watch The Text from Hell. Yes, it's a real movie."

Maria, out of breath, says, "Yes! Must have more fake blood.

Ben laughs. Tiffany says, "Ben, what've you done to my girl?"

Ben shakes his head. "I did nothing. She had the longing in her heart for stupid movies in her all along."

Tiffany and I say at the same exact time. "Nerd."

I smile because I chose the best nerd in the world.

We finish clearing the closet and end up with six donation bags full of mom's clothes. For some reason, she has three pairs of the same red cowboy boots. The boots are covered in silver stars and tiny cacti. The most ridiculous shoes I've ever seen. I'm curious as to why the person making these thought they were cute. The thought of buying three pairs is unfathomable.

"Lucy, should I wear a pair of these boots for prom?" Ben asks.

"No, please don't. I think you'd look best in the black sneakers you got for your birthday last year. These boots are so embarrassing. Mom could win a prize for the worst shoes of all time." I giggle with Ben.

He takes off his black tennis shoes and replaces them with the boots. When he's putting them on, he smiles. "Howdy, partner. How're you doin', lil' lady? Oh, man Luce, these are comfy! You know what I need?"

I have the most ridiculous boyfriend. But, he takes me out of my head when I need it the most. I mean, if you can't find humor in things, is life worth it?

"I know I need a new boyfriend. Those shoes are distracting me from having any thoughts. Please, take them off!"

Ben laughs so hard, he snorts. In his worst southern accent, he says, "Well, this cowboy needs a hat. Let us go fetch one in the old waterin' hole, my lady. Maybe we can ride on my horse into the sunset."

I roll my eyes and turn away. "Wow. Please stop. I'm so glad you don't have a Southern accent. I don't think I could be seen in public with you."

"Your loss. I look awesome."

The front door slams. Tiffany and Maria must be back. They were putting up posters to advertise our address for the garage sale. I hear the keys rattle on the kitchen table and the fridge open.

Tiffany comes into the room. "Do you guys want a strawberry margarita? I won't add any tequila to yours."

Ben smiles. "Yes, I'd love one. We deserve it. We worked hard today."

"I've never had one. But, the idea of them sounds perfect to me. I love sour things and slushies. Can I have extra ice?"

Tiffany replies, "Yes, of course. I love extra ice too."

"I just realized something," I tell Ben.

"What is it, Lucy?"

"I want tacos. Should we make some?"

Maria screams excitedly from the kitchen, "Tacos sound super great! But I'm not eating anything vegetarian. Sorry, Luce, I was raised with meat on everything."

I walk into the kitchen. "It's okay. If you want to continue the killing of harmless animals for your own selfish consumption, that's totally your choice. It won't be mine. Working in the meat department at Smiles has opened my eyes even more of how gross meat is. It doesn't help that I get grossed out by blood. Even more so now."

Maria pours ice into the blender. "I understand, LL. Sorry if I was rude. I just hate tofu. Too slimy."

"Lucy, don't let her fool you," Tiffany says. "Maria lives off grilled cheese, chicken nuggets, and pepperoni pizza. She eats like a child."

Maria walks over and kisses her. "Hush you. You don't know me. I'm going to keep kissing you, so you don't reveal all my secrets."

"Well, I'm not lying to my niece and saying you eat elaborate meals that incorporate your awesome Filipino heritage. Now, we all know you're all about eating like a first-grader"

"Ha-ha, Tiff. Not everyone likes kale. Kale rhymes with fail, so obviously no one should eat it."

Ben comes into the kitchen and is super enthusiastic. "Guys, I have a good idea! While you were all in here talking, I put some lawn chairs on the patio. I figured we could sit outside. I know Lucy always says she wants to spend more time in the backyard. Besides, what sounds better than relaxing with some margaritas together?"

"Ben, that's music to my ears," Maria says. "I wanted to sit outside anyway before we watched the next horror movie. Let me blend these up and I'll meet you guys out there."

Tiffany opens the cupboards, looking for glasses. "Great call. See you outside."

Snowball follows us through the sliding glass door. Without delay, the Arizona humidity sticks to the back of my neck.

Get me out of here.

I hope Chuck comes home soon. He deserves to relax, too.

Maria comes outside with the strawberry margaritas. "Here you go, Ben. Lucy, I put extra lime juice in yours. Let me know what you think."

I take a drink and immediately regret it while coughing. "Um, I think I got the wrong one. I'm pretty sure this has alcohol in it." The tequila burns my throat.

Maria grabs it and takes a sip. "Yep, this one's definitely mine. Sorry about that."

We switch glasses and I drink it so fast I get a brain freeze. I lay down in my chair and a part of me thinks about how fearful I've been of everything lately. Am I capable of making it through? I've never done anything without my mom being there in the background. I mean, I've always been pretty self-sufficient, but she was still in my life somehow. It sucks, living like an orphan. I hate going back and forth about how I feel.

Fuck being bipolar. I know I'm supposed to say it doesn't define me, but in moments like this, it does.

My phone vibrates on the table. I wonder who's calling.

Ben looks at the screen. "Lucy, it's Rosa. That's strange. Why would she be calling you? Were we on schedule today?"

"No, the store's not even officially open again yet. I know Chuck went in. Maybe he wanted her help. I don't know." I get up from my chair. I don't want to answer it but something inside is telling me this is important. "Hey, Rosa, how are you?"

"I'm fine, but Chuck isn't. He's been on aisle three all morning crying and he's refusing to leave. He's saying that you're the only one who understands what's going on. Can you come down here?"

"Yes, I'll be there soon. Stay safe."

"Thank you, Lucy. I miss Raymond, too, so I don't think I'm the best person for Chuck right now. I'm grieving as much as him."

"I understand. See you in 10 minutes." I say and hang up.

"What?" Ben asks.

"Well, being in the store hit him harder than he thought. Apparently, Chuck is crying and refusing to leave aisle three. I think I'm going to head down there and check in with him."

Tiffany says, "Do you want us to go with you?"

"No, thanks. I think I need to do this one alone. I'll be back later."

Ben says, "Well, hurry back. Try and remember everything Dr. Prince taught you. You don't want to be crying with him, too. He needs your strength."

"I just have Chuck's fate in my hands. No pressure or anything."

"You'll be great, Lucy." Ben says and kisses my forehead.

I find the keys to mom's black sedan and head to the store.

I want to listen to music and just scream right now. But, I think that driving without music will keep my brain calm. Staying calm is going to be key in helping Chuck.

Even though I feel like a child, there's nothing wrong with me. I love and accept myself completely.

Even though I feel like a child, there's nothing wrong with me. I love and accept myself completely.

CHAPTER FOURTEEN

W hile I drive I try putting myself in Chuck's shoes. We haven't been to the store since the incident. What would make him feel better right now? My mind wanders back to that day. We got chocolate milk and powdered sugar donuts. The two of those are just what he needs.

I make a detour towards Lucky Liquor.

The familiar bell rings as I enter and I head straight for the fridge to grab two chocolate milks and spin down the snack aisle to find the donuts. There is no time for small talk today.

"Lucy! So good to see you. I haven't seen you and Chuck for weeks. Everything okay?"

"Yep, all good." I say while swiping my card.

The transaction is approved and I don't stay to talk. Like I said, no time.

I finally make it to the store and park in the back. For a second, I wonder where Raymond's car is, but then I'm greeted with the confirmation that I'll never see his car again.

I go through the back doors and immediately come upon Rosa.

"Lucy! Thank you so much. I figured you'd be the best person for him right now. You were here the day Raymond was found."

"Yep, no problem Rosa. I'm on it." I say while the plastic bag full of sugar crinkles as I walk.

I do the vagus nerve breathing that Dr. Prince taught me. I find myself in a better state than I thought possible, so I head towards Chuck, ignoring the meat department I walk to aisle three.

All of the apples have been cleared out, don't know why I thought the body might still be here. All that remains now is a chalk outline of Raymond, a few apples scattered around with traces of blood, and some caution tape bunched on the ground.

Chuck's on his knees and screaming. "Why? Why did this have to happen?"

I'm immediately reminded of the day that happened and go sit next to him. I open one of the chocolate milks and put it in front of him. I don't bother him, but just wait for him to notice I'm here.

A few minutes go by and he acknowledges that I'm next to him. He jumps, "Lucy! When did you get here?"

"I didn't want to bother you, so I've just been sitting and hoping that you'd be okay."

He opens the chocolate milk and says, "Any donuts?"

I hand him the package and say, "Of course. No better combination."

"Thanks, Lucy. I didn't think today was going to be so hard."

I look closely at his eyes and notice the lingering tears. His face looks pained every time he attempts to smile. I feel bad for him.

I put my arm around him and say, "What's going on?"

"Well, I came down to get the store organized to open and I just broke down again. I honestly had been preparing myself for this, so—" He looks around like it's all new to him. "I don't even know what happened."

"You could prepare all you want, but it's going to be a while until we both feel at peace with it. You lost your dad by your girlfriend killing him. This isn't normal, dude."

In the last few weeks, I feel like I've matured like 20 years. Some of the stuff I say lately doesn't feel like it's coming from me.

"Do you think we should have a funeral for him or something?"

"I don't know. That's up to you. We had one for my grandpa earlier and it was just Tiffany, Maria, Ben, and I. I liked it because I could cry and not be worried about what other people think since it was all family. I also didn't wear black because I don't think that's a happy color."

My mind is feeling too much about the two deaths, I begin thinking of the color black. Why do we wear black on funerals? Is it because black is the color of crows? Why couldn't people choose a better color like green? I know that when I die people better wear orange or something.

I think I'm getting manic.

I see Chuck's gray beard.

I see some Granny Smith apples.

I see my yellow tennis shoes.

"Why did he have to die, Lucy? We were just starting to get along. I thought I was developing a relationship with him for once. Just the day before, he had sent me a text saying he was proud of me."

"It sucks that he's dead, but there's nothing we can do about it now. Maybe we should find you a therapist or something. I'm still learning to deal with things, so I'm not going to be much of a help. Let's have a funeral for him. I think that may help."

"A small funeral sounds nice. I don't think I can do a eulogy or something in front of people. Especially the ones we work with. Besides, after my 40th birthday, I'm embarrassed to be around anyone from the store. I just want to be alone while I officially say goodbye to him."

"Why would you be embarrassed?"

A little bit of reflection leads me back to that day. Chuck passing out, the stale alcohol on my mom's breath, and the way everyone left in a flash.

"Lucy, don't play dumb. I was a complete idiot and made myself look unprofessional. Bosses don't pass out drunk. I want to make people excited to come back to work. By doing that, I need to take action and take back my life. I've decided I'm going to stop drinking."

My eyes light up. I have been looking forward to him and mom's sobriety for as long as I can remember. Could this be true?

"You? You're not going to drink at all anymore?"

"Not even a sip. I need to be a better role model for you and the store. My dad may be gone, but I need to keep it together. It's what he would've wanted."

"You're right. The store was his life. That's probably a little intimidating, but you can definitely do it. Let's honor him later, okay?"

"That's a good idea. Let's have a formal goodbye."

"Yes, on one condition, though."

"Anything you want, Lucy."

"No black! Black is so depressing and I think your dad would want us to dress in green or something."

"Agreed. Let me arrange for some things to get the blood out of here and the store sparkling again. I'll be home later."

"Good idea. Blood would be probably off putting for customers. I'm going to go home and get some stuff together. See you when I see you."

He goes in for a bear hug and says, "Love you."

"Love you, too. Wait, one more thing."

"What is it?"

"The day of your birthday party, did you hit mom? She showed me her black eye and said it was from you. I enjoy us getting so close, but I'm also a little scared. I mean, would you hit me?"

"Your mom had a black eye? Are you serious?"

"Yeah…"

"Well, it definitely wasn't from me. Promise. I wanted to marry her. I would never hit her."

Chuck wanted to marry her? That's shocking based on how much she called him an idiot and a loser. Love makes you crazy I guess. I know I believe him. This was a big thing to lie about. Mom's crazier than I thought.

"Okay, thanks for telling me the truth. We have been getting closer and stuff, so I figured I should tell you the truth."

"I appreciate that. You can come to me any time."

"Thanks, love you. Are you going to be okay?"

"Yeah, I think so. Thanks, Lucy."

I try to find Rosa to say bye, but can't find her anywhere.

I make my way back home and smile. I think I helped Chuck feel better which is all I hoped for. Most people just need someone there to listen to them and feel less alone.

I pull into the driveway and see that the rental car is still here.

Thank god.

In the air-conditioned house, I'm immediately greeted by the smell of tacos. Onions and tomatoes fill the air. I should probably eat something that's real food and not sugar.

I hear laughter coming from outside. I'm so glad that I was able to leave Ben and not worry about him.

"Hey, y'all. Glad to see someone put food on the stove. I'm starving."

Ben runs over, "My love! How is everything? Was Chuck passed out or something?"

"No. He was just upset. Aisle three is going to hold a lot of memories for us for the rest of our lives. I just let him cry and talk everything out."

"Good. I'm sure he needed someone who fully understands. I mean I can try, but I never saw the dead body."

"How are you doing, though? Ever since we had that fight, I'm trying to remember you have emotions, too. I tend to get buried in mine and think that the world revolves around me."

"I know. You do take things too personally, Lucy, but that doesn't make you a bad person. I'm doing fine. We definitely missed you."

I see Tiffany and Maria dancing together singing along to some music that's in Spanish. A part of me wants to let them know that I'm back, but they are too cute. I don't want to stop this moment for them.

I go to grab a sip of Ben's margarita and the fire alarm goes off.

I rush to the kitchen and see that the pan of tomatoes and onions is burning. The kitchen's filling up with smoke. I turn the pan off and throw it in the sink.

Maria runs in, "Oh, my goodness! What happened?"

The smoke fills my eyes and they start watering. I'm so glad I caught this. It could've been a lot worse.

"It's no problem. I figured it out. But, I don't know what we're going to do for dinner now."

"Well, looks like we are going to have to go out to eat."

I'm happy to know that I didn't have to add the house burning down to the list of tragedies in my life. I definitely would not be able to handle that.

Well, where does everyone want to go?" I ask.

"Well, what would you like, Ben? I'm full of donuts and chocolate milk. Real food is necessary."

Ben puts his hand on his chin, looking like a professor. "Hmm, I'm craving sushi. We should go to that place where they cook the food in front of you. he one on Harbor and First."

A light bulb goes off in my head. "Yes, I remember. Tokyo Time! Let me get dressed really quick."

I put some teal leggings on and leave my Snowball fur-infested black shirt on. I slide my black flats on and proceed to walk to the living room, where I kiss Snowball goodbye. Maria snatches the keys and we shut the door behind us in a high that can only be described as enormous love.

We reach the rental car and Ben says, "Hand me the keys, Tiffany. You or Maria can't drive right now. You've been drinking all day. I'm not about to have one of you get a DUI."

Tiffany says, "Yes, good idea. I can barely feel the alcohol in my body, but I agree. Better safe than sorry."

I pull my phone out and text Chuck, *"Hey dude. We're going to Tokyo Time for dinner. Let me know if you want to meet us or not. We can save a seat for you."*

He responds right away, *"Thanks for the offer, but I have too much going on here. We may have to postpone the memorial for my dad till tomorrow. Have fun."*

"No worries. We can do it whenever you feel comfortable. See you later."

Like sardines, we all pile into the convertible. Ben speeds away leaving the house like a bolt of lightning. I feel a little car sick.

"Wow! You're enjoying driving this car, huh?" I say while my hair fans on my face.

"Yeah! I don't know why I never drove one of these before. I feel like a racecar driver!" he says with a smile as big as the moon. I guess we all gotta let our guard down from time to time.

We made it to the restaurant thankfully in one piece.

We're greeted at Tokyo Time by a server named Aiko. Her eyes are full of kindness and she bows, welcoming us into the busy restaurant. Aiko stands at about four-feet-eleven and has long black hair like charcoal burning on a summer barbecue.

I tell her, "Party of four, please."

Aiko takes four laminated menus and leads the way to the four chairs and stove that will be used to cook or dinner. Ben and I order tofu and vegetables, while Maria and Tiffany go for steak and lobster.

Our chef for the night, Robert, shows up. He's wearing a red chef's hat and a white coat that looks like he's about to do some science experiments. "Hello, everyone. Welcome to Tokyo Time. How are you all doing?"

Tiffany puts her arm around Ben. "We're here to celebrate these two teenagers right here! They're graduating high school next week!"

Everyone at our table claps for him, including a family of three with a little boy.

Ben turns red, resembling a ripe tomato. Robert starts cooking and it's so fun watching him. He makes a volcano out of onions and a rooster out of egg yolk. There's something oh so soothing and fascinating about watching your dinner get cooked in front of you.

Tiffany whispers to me, "Hey, Luce, I've noticed Ben's a little embarrassed, so I'll lay off putting attention on him."

Ben whispers back, "I can hear you guys, ya know." Maria drinks some red wine with a huge smile while she watches Robert cook.

Tiffany looks at her and says, "Babe, should we ask her now?"

"Ask me what?" I reply. They look at each other and laugh. Is there something I missed in my state of zoning out lately? I dart my eyes back and forth between them in hopes of an answer. "What's up, guys? Is everything okay? Did I do something wrong…?"

Tiffany giggles. "No, of course not. There's just something I've been meaning to talk to you about."

"Okay…"

Tiffany lets out a huge sigh. "Lucy, will you be my maid of honor? I wanted to ask your mom because I know she'd make it a big deal if I didn't. But, judging by how close you and I have gotten, it seems like a no brainer."

I gasp. "Yes, of course. I'd be honored. Do I have to wear a certain color dress or anything? What does this mean? Do I have to plan a bachelorette party?"

"No, you don't have to wear a certain color or anything. Just a costume. My friends are most likely going to plan something. You're under twenty-one anyway, so I feel like anything you plan wouldn't work out, if you get what I mean."

How exciting. I've never been to someone's wedding before. Let alone be in one! I can't believe she thought to ask me. I blush and eat my teriyaki sauce covered onions and zucchini.

"Thank you so much for thinking of me. I feel honored."

Maria puts her glass out to cheer all us. "To Lucy, the best maid of honorrrrr. Why do they call it that? It's not like you'll be wearing honor!" Ben and I hold out our water glasses to cheer. Maria giggles, which leads me to believe she's a little drunk. I've never seen her like this. Her red cheeks and huge grin are adorable.

I finish my food and tell our waitress, "Can I have some green tea ice cream, please?" Ben orders some too, while Maria orders another glass of wine.

The wine comes and Maria finishes the glass in one sip.

Maria slurs her words, "Lushy! LL! My girllll... How are you feelin'? Are you excited about graduashunnnnn? Next week, right? Wooooooooah. The room is spinning around and around."

"The idea of getting out of here fills me with so much joy. I daydream about coffee daily. Did you know there are over two hundred different coffee shops in Seattle alone?"

"Yeah! Coffee! I love coffee. I want a cup. Wait. No, I have wine! I love wine! Just like coffee."

Tiffany and Ben crack up.

Ben tries to speak through the laughs. "How much wine did you drink?"

"Not enoughhhhhh." she says while holding her glass out to get filled.

I usually hate when people drink this much, but with Maria being so funny, it doesn't seem to matter.

Tiffany looks at Maria and says, "Babe, are you going to eat any of your food? You haven't touched it."

Maria winks. "I'm going to save for later, you know what I mean. Wink wink."

"No, I don't know what that means at all. But we'll just get you a box. Also, you don't say wink out loud. Goober. You just do it."

Maria, with her purple lips, gives a thumbs-up. "Whateverrrrr you sayyyyyy."

Aiko hands me the green tea ice cream and the bill to Tiffany. "Thank you for coming to Tokyo Time. See you all soon!"

Tiffany takes the check. "Don't worry, Lucy. We got this. You'll need all the money you can get when Ben starts school. Student loans are no joke. My friend went to school for three months for her teaching credential. She still owes about nineteen thousand dollars."

"Are you serious? That's ridiculous. Did she finish?"

"No, she realized she wasn't interested in teaching anymore. Now, she's a trapeze artist in a traveling circus. Last time we talked, she was in Paris."

"We'll have to talk more about this when we get home. I don't know if Maria should drink anymore."

"Yeah, we need to get out of here before she tries to convince someone to buy her more."

Tiffany knows Maria best.

Maria seriously just asked the woman next to her. "Hey stranger, wanna share a bottle of wine?"

The lady in the pink shirt looks confused. "I'm sorry, ma'am. I don't usually drink with people I don't know. I hope you understand."

Ben tells the lady, "Don't worry about it. She's had too much to drink tonight anyway."

Maria groans. "Come on, Benny. Big Ben. My dude. I thought we were nerdy buddies."

"Oh, Maria. We still are. I just don't want you to be hungover tomorrow. That doesn't sound like very fun. Now, come on. We're going home."

Maria stands up from the wooden chair and says, "Goodbye, everyone. I love you all."

We walk through the dark parking lot and the star filled sky is beautiful. The stars look like diamonds smiling down on me. As cheesy as it sounds, looking at the night sky always makes me feel better. All of the galaxies surrounding the sky remind me that there's a world out there that's bigger than me. I'm just a speck in this beautiful planet.

CHAPTER FIFTEEN

en and I slide into the backseat and Maria plops down in the front seat.

"Are you sure you can drive, Tiffany?" Ben asks.

"Yes, thanks for asking. I drank a whole bunch of water and I only had one drink earlier. It's worn off by now."

"Okay. If you end up not feeling safe, let me know." Ben says. "I can drive."

Tiffany puts her seat belt on and puts the keys in the ignition. "Babe, put your seat belt on please."

"Yes, yes. Safety first. I wanna sing!" Maria shouts.

I don't think she knows the volume of her voice at the moment. She clicks in her metal seat belt and scrolls through the radio stations, finally landing on a country song with the most Texas accent I've ever heard. *"All I need is my wife. These country roads and this guitar. I put that ring on her finger. The rest is our little history. Me and her until the afterlife."*

While singing along, Maria puts her hand out with the ring on her finger.

"He's singing about us, T! You put a ring on my finger. All we need now is a guitar!"

Before any of us say anything, she starts crying. She's ridiculous.

Ben rolls his eyes and says, "Of all the songs to cry to Maria, you chose the most redneck one on the radio."

"Don't let her accent fool you, Ben. She is a redneck at heart."

While tears fall down her face, she clutches my hand. "Lucy, I love you. Growing up in the Philippines, I never thought I'd be where I am now. I met your aunt and then you. Lucky me. I love you!"

"I'm lucky that you're in my life now. I love you, too."

The country music plays on the way home. I may hate this music, but I love this family of mine.

We make it home and Chuck's car still isn't in the driveway. I hope everything is going alright at the store and he's feeling better. Maria stumbles through the door and Snowball rushes by.

"Guyssssss, didddd you seeee that? A white creature made it into the house! I think it's an albino squirrel or something?" she says.

"That's just Snowball, Maria. You're fine."

"But, she looked like a big marshmallow!!! I need some water."

I'm so appreciative of the fact that Maria knows when to stop drinking. I guess alcohol isn't all bad when you know how to limit yourself.

I grab Maria a glass of water who's sitting at the table with Tiffany and Ben. "I drank wayyyy too much. Why didn't anyone say anything?" Maria says.

"Well, you looked like you were having fun. I also asked Lucy to be my maid of order, so we were all just having a good time." Tiffany says.

"Okay, good to know at least one good thing happened tonight." she says while finishing the glass of water.

"Well, Lucy, I know you probably want to go to bed, but I realized that there's one thing I don't know about you."

"Okay…" I say while panicking.

Does she think I murdered Raymond? Is she paying bail to get mom back?

"What are you doing after high school graduation? We've been so wrapped up in your mom. I don't even think I've asked you yet."

"That's funny because the only thing I've been thinking about lately is getting out of here. Not the full details of everything that's on the horizon."

"I can understand that. Out with it, girl!"

"Well, Ben and I are both going to Seattle Central. It's a community college and will hopefully save us a lot of money. Ben has an idea of what he wants to do career wise and I don't. I don't want to spend thousands of dollars for general education on loans I'll never be able to pay off."

"Ben, you already know what you're thinking about for a career?! That's amazing!"

Ben says, "Yeah, I do. At first I thought engineering, but then I thought I'd get bored of that. But, then one day Lucy said I'm good at seeing both sides of an argument and calming people down. So, I'm thinking like a foreign diplomat or something like that."

"Wow! That's amazing. Do you know other languages?"

"Actually, I do. I have this app on my phone called Language Limbo and I'm pretty good at Spanish now. I've already started Mandarin…"

Before Ben can talk about the fact that he wants to learn Italian, French, Russian, and at least five others, Maria says, "I'll teach you Tagalog! You'd love it and get it straight from the source."

"Mahal Kita, Maria! I'd love that."

I say, "Does this mean you've been practicing Tagalog, too? You never cease to amaze me." I say.

"Yeah! Ever since Maria got here, I've been trying to learn a few things. Mahal Kita means I love you. I figured that would be a good one to know since she's family." Maria kisses his cheek and starts crying. Again.

"Oh, Ben. No one has said that to me since I left over 20 years ago. My family stopped speaking to me when I told them I was a lesbian."

I attempt to prevent a sob fest and the usual dramatics that come with alcohol.

"Don't worry, Maria! We love you! We'll be cheering the whole wedding."

Ben goes along with my statement of positivity, "Yes! We love you, Auntie! Can I show you something on the tv?"

Tiffany mouths *'thank you'* to Ben and I. Ben leads her to the tv while I get her more water.

I hear Ben from the kitchen. "So, Maria, this is a show called *The Crazy Comic Corners*. It's all about a guy who sells and collects comic books. His shop is here in Arizona."

I sit on the couch and say, "It's a great show. Especially the host with the long white beard, Bud Lightning."

Tiffany says, "You watch this, too? Wow, Ben, you've made everyone nerds in this house! You'll never convert me, though. What kind of name is Bud Lightning?"

"I don't think his real name's Bud Lightning, but it sounds pretty cool. He has gone to places like London and Manhattan interviewing people obsessed with them. One lady from Germany had a whole collection in an entire room in her house! She had over ten thousand! She also had character tattoos covering her arms. It was amazing."

The door opens and I hear Chuck's voice. "Are you all watching *The Crazy Comic Corners* without me?"

"You know about *this* show, Chuck? This is my worst nightmare. Being surrounded by nerds. When's the alien ship coming to get us, Ben?"

Chuck says, "I love this show! Bud Lightning is totally my main crush. Ben showed this to me, but I collected a lot of comics when I was a kid. I wish I had saved some of mine."

After watching a full episode, Maria, out of breath, says, "Can we go to a comic bookstore tomorrow, Tiff? I want to start a collection just like the people on the show!"

Ben high-fives her. "Yes! Oh, wait. I'll be at school. I can write down some names of a few that are kinda close to here."

Tiffany says, "Thanks a lot, Ben. We're supposed to be saving for our wedding. Remember, Maria?"

Maria winks. "But, comics are such a good investment. Some people on the show have some that are worth over a thousand dollars!"

Everyone in this house is so crazy. Including me who forgot about going back to school tomorrow.

I get up from the couch and say, "Good night, everyone. I'm going to bed. My senior year awaits me in the morning. I love you all."

"Good night, Lucy!" everyone says and I give them a thumbs up.

While I grab a cup for water, I see Chuck pull a six pack out of the fridge. I thought he had stopped drinking. I don't say anything because it's not my life even though a part of me is bummed about it.

He snaps one open and pours it down the sink with the other 5. My hand stops gripping the cup so tight and a smile peeks out. Thank god.

"Before I forget, Chuck! I dumped mom's clothes on the floor in your room. I'm sorry!"

He turns around and faces me, "What do you mean? Why would you do that?"

"I didn't want to look at her stuff anymore and was thinking we could have a garage sale…"

"Oh, okay. Good idea. I was thinking of doing something similar soon."

"So, you're not mad?"

"No. I do wish you would've talked to me about it."

"I was thinking of calling you and asking for your opinion. But, I didn't want to bother you and I was just getting annoyed seeing her stuff everywhere."

"I understand, but remember that you're not the only one going through this. She was *my* girlfriend for years and I don't know how to even get her out of my head. I'm so lost."

Tiffany comes up and says, "I'm mostly sober. Do you wanna talk?"

"That would actually be nice. I have no friends that are sober."

"Okay, well, you two enjoy yourselves. I'm going to attempt to relax."

"Lucy, be sure to clear enough space for me in my room, so I can actually sleep in there."

"Okay, sounds good. Wait! One more thing! Did everything work out at the store?All the blood gone now?"

"Yep. We should be open by Friday! Rosa helped a lot. I completely understand what my dad saw in her."

"Awesome! See you tomorrow."

I move all of mom's clothes and shoes to one corner of the room. All of her clothes have her familiar smell of vodka, cigarettes, and sour candy. All that's left of mom now is her smell. I run out of the room, so I don't find myself randomly sad or upset about something out of my control. Sadly, my default mood has become sadness with her gone.

I take my pills and lay in my bed. I make sure my alarm is set for 7:00 tomorrow, so I can get to school okay. I start to freak out, but try to remember what coping strategies Dr. Prince and I went over last time. My mantra should help.

Even though I feel like a child, there's nothing wrong with me. I love and accept myself completely.

Even though I feel like a child, there's nothing wrong with me. I love and accept myself completely

Waking up to loud birds singing their songs and sweat leaving its mark on my back isn't what I had planned for this Wednesday morning. Living in this desert feels like my blood could boil any minute and I want to just shave off all my hair. I always say I want to cut it, but I know I'd miss it. My face wouldn't be able to pull off the bald look anyway.

As I get up , I notice Ben's still snoring. We usually leave by 7:30 and it's already 7:05.

I shake him. "Ben, wake up. It's time for school!"

He rolls over and faces the wall. "I don't want to go. Wake me up in five minutes."

I go into the bathroom, wash my face, and look in the mirror. My eyes are full of color. I haven't seen this much color in them for a long time. Guess a good night of sleep can make a huge difference.

With this new mindset of positivity, I grab my backpack without a feeling of dread of going to school. It helps that this is the last week we have to be there until 3:00. Starting next week, we only have to be there until 12:00! My last week of high school, I'm sure it will be pretty easy. Right?

"Ben! Wake up!" I say this for the second time.

"Fineeeee." He sprouts out of bed. I make sure to take my meds and make my way to the kitchen. I make some toast for us.

Ben walks in with his hair in three different directions. He's wearing what he had on yesterday. He doesn't care about what he looks like or even what people think of him. I've always admired that because I get upset even when someone looks at me funny.

I hand him two pieces of buttered toast.

"Thanks. It's almost our last week of hell school! I mean, high school! You ready?"

"Not even close." Ben grabs his backpack from the closet and I put mine over my shoulder. He drives us to school and a big part of me is ready to go home.

Ben walks me to my first class, English with Mr. Phelps. I hope today goes fast. These two remaining weeks of senior year seriously sound like a huge waste of time. I'm sure some people are going to be sad knowing they won't see each other for a while, but I couldn't be happier to not see some of them ever again. Especially Rebecca Gardner. I hate her.

Rebecca and I used to be friends when we were kids. In 6th grade, she copied off a test in history class and the teacher blamed me. but she always claimed it was me that cheated and not her. She also got boobs in like 5th grade

She is standing in the doorway using her phone camera as a mirror.

"Excuse me, please." I say while squeezing my stomach in to get inside.

"Eww, if it isn't Murder Girl. You've been gone so long I thought your mom killed you, too." she says while smacking her pink lipgloss.

Everyone stops talking and just stare right at me. My anxiety usually makes me feel like everyone is looking at me, but right now I know they are for sure.

I search for the right words which just end up turning into stutters. "What...areee...you talkinnnggg about?"

"Oh, Lucy. Stop acting so naive. I know your mom killed that guy at the store or whatever. Julio told me. He said that your mom is in jail now and is teaching you how to murder people. Like a family business."

"What are you even talking about Rebecca? The store has been closed for a while. Someone did die, but that's also not your business. So, if you don't mind, please shut up." Lauren says while coming to my rescue.

Note to self, buy Lauren a cape. Also, punch Julio. I don't know why I didn't think of him sooner. He's Rosa's son and the biggest loud-mouth I've ever met.

"I know it's none of my business. I figured as class president all, everyone would want to know that a murderer is at school. I mean, I'm not scared of Lucy, but that's just because I listen to a lot of serial killer podcasts. I have a lot of skills in defending myself."

This rivalry or whatever you want to call it started between Rebecca and I when we were in 2nd grade. She may be crazy, but she can hold a grudge like nobody's business. "You don't have to defend yourself against me. I have no desire to kill anyone."

"Good. I would hate to be murdered by someone so ugly and boring."

Mr. Phelps walks in while I feel my eyes getting wet. I'm not going to give her the satisfaction of crying in front of her. I run to my seat and pull out my reusable water bottle. I take a few sips to avoid making eye contact with anyone right now.

Mr. Phelps then spends the rest of the period telling us stories about his experiences at college. He tells us all about how he'd sit at the library drinking cappuccinos and digging through the old books on art history. Mr. Phelps or Jeff (what he wants us to call him now since "we're all friends") wanted to be a professor of art history for a long time. It wasn't until his last year of college that he realized he wanted to help high schoolers. I don't know where the story is even going, but it does leave me with a good reminder.

It's okay to not have everything figured out yet. I've spent a lot of time worrying about mom lately. Time to ignore bitches like Rebecca for the next week and to take that time back for myself.

The bell rings and Lauren makes sure to be at my desk, so I don't walk out alone.

We reach the hallway and she says, "I hate her. Why did she think saying all of that is even okay? She's such a dumb bitch."

"She's just insecure or something. I don't know." I'm trying not to dwell on what she told the entire class. I wouldn't be surprised if right now she's finding more minions to spread lies to.

Ben walks up and says, "Who's insecure? I mean we're in high school, so the probability of that is pretty high. I've also noticed that our generation uses a lot of filters in photos of themselves which most likely adds to that insecurity. I know that I refuse..."

Lauren says, "I love the social commentary and all, but I'm just trying to check in with Lucy. Rebecca told the whole class that Lucy is a murderer and that any of us could be next."

"Are you fucking serious? Where is she? I need to have a chat with her right away." Ben says while he laughs like a villain and turns as red as a stop sign.

I push him back and say, "Just stop. She's not worth it. Besides, I have to go to math class."

In math class, my phone vibrates. I dash it away, so Mrs. Connor doesn't take it away. I zip it in my front pocket, but it vibrates again. I hope everyone is okay. I carefully put my phone in my pocket and ensure no one notices.

I raise my hand. "Mrs. Connor, can I use the bathroom?" She says yes and hands me the bathroom pass, which is actually an Arizona license plate. The license plate is a little much, but no one has stolen it yet. So, she has the right idea.

I head down the hallway and look at my phone. The texts are from Chuck. *"Hey, Lucy, how are you doing? Just realized you're at school."*

"Don't respond. Meet me at Smiles after work. Love you."

"Dude! I was so scared. I'm glad you're okay. I'll see you later." I reply and head back to class.

I was right. School was annoying and worthless. All my classes were so boring. All I learned was that teachers seem to want to give more advice as their time with you becomes less. The most interesting thing to happen all day was a girl in my history class got her phone taken away.

I walk to my black sedan after my last class in hopes that Ben will be here soon. As I scroll through my phone to make time go faster on Instaphoto, I see selfies of people with the hashtag Class of 2021. Why are hashtags popular? I don't want to be a downer, but they're stupid and don't make any sense.

Ben puts his hand on my phone screen. "Ready to see more than just people on your phone screen? Let's go!"

Thank goodness. I started to get a little sad that no one took a selfie with me yet. It's crazy how apps on a phone can make you feel alone and a waste of time. We get into the black car and turn the ice cold air-conditioner on then head over to Smiles.

As we walk through the doors, I recognize customers and bend my head so none of them see me. I make sure to avoid aisle three as much as possible. I hate being here. I hear footsteps coming toward me. I've been spotted. Shit.

Please don't be a customer.

Julio looks at me and then at the Winter Roar. "Stealing, McBride? Wouldn't want anyone to see you. What are you doing here anyway?"

I look at his grease filled hair and smell his cologne. I swear he has a trail of it following him. He's even wearing the dumb, yellow work shirt.

"Eww, go away. Please go bother someone else. Wait, what are *you* doing here?"

He crosses his arms, "I work here now. Since you're hiding away and having a pity party, my mom asked Chuck if I could have a job. He obviously said yes."

I say, "I didn't realize Chuck was so desperate. I guess he'll just hire anyone." And turn my back towards him.

"Don't go murdering anyone now, McBride." Julio shouts.

CHAPTER SIXTEEN

I notice veins popping through Ben's neck. "He's not worth our time."

Ben says, "I wish I could turn around and punch that dumb smile off his face."

"Right there with you. However, the store just opened again and I don't want to worry customers. Punching him may be even further proof that I'm violent."

We arrive at Chuck's office and hear him on the phone, "Yes, that would be great. The biggest sandwich tray you have. Make sure there's a lot of veggies! My daughter is vegetarian. See you in an hour."

I hear him hang up and knock on the door, "Chuck, can we come in?"

"Of course. Ordering a sandwich tray for the crew. Everyone's been here since 5 AM!" he says.

He spins around in his chair. His smile is wide enough to make my heart soar with warmth. I haven't seen him this happy in a long time.

"So, how are you?" I ask.

"Great, Lucy. I worked like crazy yesterday. I had to throw away a lot of stuff that had spoiled and everything. I also hired a clean up crew who got rid of all the blood. I even had a little ceremony for dad on aisle three. Just me and him." he says while biting his lip.

"Oh? I'm sorry I missed it. How did that go?"

"Hard. I didn't think I'd miss him as much as I do. We had so many unresolved issues we never worked through. I know I'll never stop missing him. He loved you a lot, too Lucy."

What do I say back to that? Raymond was just a weird grandpa figure in my life. He wasn't that nice or even my blood family.

For Chuck's sake, I say, "I loved him, too. He was a good store owner. Now, what's going on? Your text made it seem like there was something important happening."

"You're right. There is an issue we need to discuss. I was hoping to talk to you about it. But alone. We won't be too long, Ben."

Ben says, "Of course. Did I do something wrong? We're cool, right?"

"Yeah, of course! We're cool." Ben walks out and I find myself weirdly anxious about this entire conversation.

"So, Lucy, there's something I've been meaning to ask you for a while. You're not in trouble or anything, okay?"

"Okay… You're not dying or something, right?"

I cross my fingers behind my back. This little act of wishing will unlikely help, but who knows? Maybe it will.

"I want you to run Smiles with me, Lucy. You could be second in command! We can make this store a family again. What do you think?"

Run Smiles with him? He can't be serious. Chuck knows that I've been planning on moving to Seattle for the last 2 years. Before Raymond's murder, it's all I talked and thought about.

"Uhh, I don't know. I mean Ben and I have been planning on going to Seattle for a while… I've been wanting to do that for a long time."

"I understand that. Customers just know you and I think you'd be such a good manager. My dad wanted to keep this store in the family for as long as possible. "

He had to go for the family angle. As much as I can understand where he's coming from, I want to continue my dreams of moving and starting my own life. I've lived in Arizona for too long and I'm ready for a change. I also have to think of his side, too. Seattle is always going to be there and he's always been there for me. I know for sure that the store would be successful with me in charge, too. I could also save a lot of money.

I find myself daydreaming both scenarios. I feel guilty for wanting to start my own life. I also know that most people dream of owning their own store. I don't know what to do. I thought I had it all figured out.

"Can I tell you in a few days? This all feels like a lot right now."

"Yes, of course. Try not to stress about it. I know you'll make the right decision."

"Okay, see you later." I say and walk out of his office.

The last 2 weeks of high school were supposed to be easy. I guess this is what life is. Expecting the unexpected. I wish I could just fast forward. The pain of the unknown is making my heart feel like it's being split in two.

The day's finally come.

Prom is here. After much contemplation, I've realized two things. I'm in charge of my moods (most of the time), so I should try and make it happy. Additionally, Prom is probably going to be a lot of fun.

Maria and Tiffany have been here since I woke up this morning. They brought donuts over for us to enjoy while we get ready.

Maria comes into the kitchen, "Lucy, how are you feeling? Have everything you need?"

"I'm okay. I'm choosing my mood today and it's feeling good. Lauren and Sarah are coming over soon. The idea of them wanting to put a bunch of makeup on me and style my hair— it honestly makes me feel a little sick to my stomach. My mom always tried to morph me into someone who did all that. I hate all of it."

"I totally get that. I used to be like you. I never wanted to spend much time on my appearance until I realized it's a great form of self-love. My only advice is don't be afraid to tell them what you want."

Maria is right. I'm just always scared of the consequences of speaking my mind. I always think I'll hurt someone's feelings.

"Good point. I'm going to take a shower. I'll see you—"

Before I finish my sentence, Tiffany says, "Be more confident! They're not going to hate you for telling them how you feel. Turn those if's into when's!"

"You're right. I just don't always feel comfortable doing it."

"I understand, Lucy. It's okay. We're here for you. Old habits are hard to fix, but we'll get there."

It feels comforting knowing that people understand you. Understanding that sometimes keeping the peace is the only way to survive. I avoided fighting mom because I never wanted things to escalate. I wish I could go back and change things, but that's a dumb way to live and think.

I put my cereal bowl in the sink and head for the bathroom. Inside my purple shorts, my phone vibrates. I glance at it, not wanting to answer. I don't feel like talking to anyone before Sarah and Lauren get here.

I look down and it says, Arizona State Holding Cell in Perryville. What does she want? I pick up to be nice and she says, "Lucy Love! How are you? I miss you!"

I roll my eyes and say, "Hi mom. Just getting ready for Prom and stuff. What do you need?" Bring on the requests for gummy worms and cigarettes.

"Oh, baby girl! I don't need anything. I was just calling to check in. My court date is coming up. The warden or whatever was telling me it will be in two weeks. The court's been blocked up with other cases. Like, they told me about this lady who lost her kids, so she killed her husband."

"Cool, mom. Why are you telling me this?" I try to think of a reason to end our conversation, but I can't think of anything.

"I just wanted to share a crazy story with you. It should be comforting to you that I never lost custody of you. You could've ended up with a crazy family."

"That's a weird thing to be grateful about, mom. Also, try and remember that you murdered someone, too. She may have lost her kids, but murder is murder."

"You know what, Lucy? Just because you're mad that I'm in jail doesn't give you the right to be mean to me. I'm trying here. I found a lawyer and everything. I just need some clothes for my court case. I don't want to be in this gross uniform in front of a jury."

I was right. She does need something. "Mom, I'm not being mean. I'm being honest with you. You murdered Raymond, simple as that. I have to go."

"Wait…" she says and I hang up before she can say anything else.

There's so much more I wish I could've said, but I'm determined to have a good day. My old self would be nervous of the consequences for everything I just said. She's gone, though. She's behind bars, what can she do? Not my problem anymore.

I grab a clean towel from the hallway closet across from the bathroom. My anxiety is trying to make an appearance. My hands shake and my heart races while I turn on the shower to warm the room with steam. The water touches my skin and I feel my wall of panic go down the drain. I'm in charge of my feelings today.

You know what the worst part of showers are? When they're over. Most of the bitterness and frustration I have for my current situation in life went down the drain with the shampoo water. Luckily, the meds I took helped, too. I dry off the remaining water on my bare skin and wrap my hair in the red towel. I notice the time is already 11:02 a.m.

Shit.

I just want to go back to sleep. I know I need to dry my hair so it looks somewhat decent for later. I don't have a hair dryer, but I know for certain mom does.

Walking into her room again while her stuff is sprawled out feels like stepping into a different world; the walls feel cold and the carpeted floor gives my entire body chills. A world flooded with memories of a person who isn't coming back. It's almost like a haunted house.

While rushing around to avoid not being in here longer than I have to, I grab her blow dryer and shut the door behind me. I decide to dry my hair in my bathroom. The hair dryer is making my hair stick on my neck in strands. I feel sweat underneath my nose and on my forehead. Drying my hair is way harder than I thought.

Breathe in. Breathe out.

I place the hair dryer on the counter and brush out my locks. My hair's super fluffy like a sheep. How do people dry their hair like this every single day? I feel like I just walked three miles in the desert. The noise was enough to rattle my nerves completely. There's a knock on the bathroom door and I jump straight up like a kangaroo.

It's just Ben. I don't know who I thought it would be, but I couldn't be happier it's him. "Hey, Lucy, your hair looks nice like that."

"You mean you don't like it when it looks like a nest?"

"No, keep that for the birds. Aren't Lauren and Sarah supposed to be here soon? I swear you mentioned something, unless I was dreaming."

"No, you weren't. Last night, I let you know before we went to bed. They'll be here soon, but I'm ready to go back to bed."

Tiffany pokes her head in the door with a chocolate sprinkled donut in her hand. Her hair's in literally four different directions. With this look, she could totally pull off a mohawk if she ever wanted one.

She hands it to me, saying, "I know my hair is ridiculous. Didn't brush it yet. I just wanted to get here as soon as possible."

"Well, you're right it's ridiculous. Is Chuck here?"

"No, he's not. Your friends just pulled, nonetheless. They're pulling stuff from the car and being loud. Just wanted to give you a heads up."

Ben gives me a hug and grabs my hands. "You can do this. You're going to be okay. I'm going to hide in the room. Don't hate me."

I hug him back and roll my eyes. "I hate you, but I love you more. See you later."

Snowball meows a bunch and leads the way down the hallway to greet Lauren and Sarah. I'd like to think her meowing like crazy is actually her trying to tell me that everything is going to be okay.

The doorbell won't stop ringing. The two of them are desperate to come inside. I hear them gossiping through the door.

"Where is she? Does she not know we're here?" Lauren says.

"Knock on the door again. I don't think she heard us the sixth time," Sarah says in such a sarcastic tone. If you could hear someone rolling their eyes without seeing their face, that just happened.

I open the door and put my arms out with full expectations I'll be bombarded with hugs. I was right. Sarah gives me a bear hug. "Lucy! I'm so happy to see you."

Lauren peers up from her phone and gives me a one-armed hug. "Hey, Lucy, did you blow dry your hair? It looks nice. Ready to get beautiful?"

I run my hands over my flat hair. "Yes, I'm glad you like it. I'm ready to get more beautiful."

Sarah hushes Lauren. "Lucy's already beautiful, crazy. You're just going to add to it."

Lauren shakes her head and says, "Yes, you're right. Sorry, Lucy. The goal is to make your beautifulness stand out more."

They come inside to find Maria still drinking the cup of water, and Tiffany pouring herself a bowl of Tasty O's.

Tiffany salutes the three of us. "Hey, kids, glad to know you're staying out of trouble."

Sarah says, "I can't promise anything about later."

"Oh, Lucy, I'm so glad you didn't move anything off the table," Lauren says. "I definitely wouldn't want to put anything back."

She grabs four different shades of lipstick that honestly look the same to me. I can just tell you they're pink and red, but that's about it. She also grabs some glitter-filled colored eyeshadow and two tubes of mascara. Is this all for me? Sarah doesn't have any makeup on yet either. I hope she goes first.

Sarah asks me, "Where's Ben? Is he getting ready at a friend's house?"

I laugh. "No, he's hiding in our room. I think he's annoyed about having so many women around. He just decided to stay away."

"He remembers my date's a girl too, right?" Sarah says while grabbing a donut.

"I'm sure he does. He remembers everything. Speaking of dates.

Are you still excited to go with Elizabeth? What color dress is she wearing? Is she coming over here to get ready with us?"

"We are both going to red dresses. Elizabeth's getting ready with her friends. I wanted this time to be for the three of us. She also said her mom's a makeup artist or something, so you know she's going to look extra beautiful."

Lauren clears her throat. "What are you trying to say? That me doing your makeup isn't good enough?"

"No, that's not what I meant at all." Sarah gulps. "I just think her mom will have more options for colors and stuff."

Lauren pushes Sarah's arm. "You know I'm just messing around. I'm just jealous of Elizabeth's mom. I bet she has every color in the rainbow to choose from. Speaking of makeup, let's get started. Who's going to go first?"

Sarah looks down at her bare feet, "Not me..."

"Whatever, I volunteer or whatever. Might as well get it over with."

Lauren crosses her arms. "I promise it won't take long and afterwards you don't have to do anything until we leave to take pictures."

Not doing anything sounds nice, but I try to remind myself that tonight is a special night for the three of us. I also plan to make some funny faces and not smile in every photo we take later. The idea of smiling for more than five minutes sounds completely painful and not realistic to my actual feelings. I hope that doesn't ruin Lauren's idea of having such a perfect day.

Maria drops a chair in the bathroom where we stand talking. She looks so tired and her eyes have circles underneath them.

"I'm jealous of you girls going to Prom. It's going to be so fun! I want to watch you get ready, but sleep sounds way better."

"Did you not sleep last night or something?" Lauren says.

Maria shakes her head, "Barely. I stayed up all night watching *The Crazy Comic Corners*. Ben has me hooked."

"I love that show! Buzz is the best!" Sarah says.

"I don't even know what that is, but I'm guessing something nerdy. Please don't share any details, Maria. I need to get Lucy ready." Lauren says.

"Yes, m'am. I'm going to go take a nap anyway."

Lauren turns on the bright lights in the bathroom and it's like two giant spotlights land directly on my face. She puts a light purple and golden glitter eyeshadow on me, pink blush on my cheeks, and black lashes that are long enough to protect me from the rain like an umbrella.

Lauren gasps. "Wow, Lucy, you look so beautiful and elegant. How do you feel?"

She moves out of the way so I can stand up from the chair. I analyze my face in the mirror. I turn it to see the rosiness from every angle. I'm speechless of my appearance. I look nothing like myself. I hate it.

"So, what do you think? You definitely look different, but I mean that in a very good way," Sarah says.

"To be honest, I don't know what to think. I know I look okay, but a part of me feels like a clown. But, I hate clowns. Can we fix it?"

"Uh, no. That doesn't answer the question, Lucy. I worked hard," Lauren says while crossing her arms and pouting.

I reply as fast as I can to not further upset her. "Oh, no, I like it. I'm just not used to it. I don't feel like myself. I was hoping for a more natural look. Don't hate me! It looks great, but it's not *me*. I'm sorry. I hope you understand. It's not you. It's me."

"It's okay, Lucy. We aren't breaking up or something. I understand. I went a little crazy on the blush. I just love pink and thought it'd look nice on you." Lauren says apologetically, "But you're right, the more I look, the more I notice you don't look like yourself."

I grab some toilet paper, get it wet under the tap, and rub it on my contoured blush-filled face. My original skin color pops up and I feel my heartbeat slow down. I look like myself again, except for the eyelashes and bright colors on my eyelids. Much to my surprise, I like the mascara and eyeshadow.

"What do you think now?" I say.

"That's better. You look more like Lucy now. The real question is what do you think?"

"I love it. My eyes look great and I don't look neon anymore. Thank you so much."

"Of course! Sarah, it's your turn now," Lauren says with a smile.

"Oh, goody. I want lots of glitter and extra mascara if possible," Sarah says and sits down.

I play some music and the three of us laugh. I'm not entirely sure what we're laughing about, but I know I'm in good company. I'm going to miss them when I move away. Luckily, they're leaving Arizona too. I didn't want to have to come back to this desert unless it was absolutely necessary.

After Lauren finishes Sarah's makeup, Sarah looks like a goddess. Her eyes sparkle like two rubies and her skin's literally glowing. I have such beautiful friends. She bats her eyes. "Is this what being pretty feels like?"

I think for a moment. "Hmm, I'm not sure, but I think we rock it and wear it well."

Lauren puts her arms around us while we look in the bathroom mirror. I haven't felt this kind of love from friends in such a long time.

"Let's take a picture." Laure says.

CHAPTER SEVENTEEN

Since Sarah's the tallest out of us, she snaps the photo. For a second, this happy moment is framed in perfect lighting and saved forever.

I walk out of the bathroom to get us a cup of water In the kitchen, Tiffany whistles. "I'm sorry, I'm looking for my niece. Have you seen her?"

Maria, who's standing next to Tiffany, puts her hand over her mouth. "Lucy, you look beautiful!"

I hear footsteps coming down the hallway. I hope it's not Lauren. I don't want to put any more makeup on.

Luckily, it's just Ben. His mouth's in an O shape and his eyes look like they're about to pop out of his head.

"Wow, Lucy, you look insanely gorgeous. The makeup looks nice. I mean, you always look good, but the makeup is just… Wow."

"Thank you, Ben. I took some of it off at first. I started to look like I should be making balloon animals at kids birthday parties."

"You're so funny. Jokes aside, I still think you look breathtaking. Are you going to do something fancy with your hair too? I noticed you washed it. Props on that one."

I get frustrated sometimes on how much he knows me. Washing my hair when I'm depressed is rare.

"Lucy, will you come in here please?" Lauren shouts from the bathroom.

I roll my eyes. "Sorry, Ben, I'm being summoned."

Ben hides away in the bedroom again while I go find out what's going on. I don't feel like dealing with anything else today.

"What's going on?"

Lauren guides her hand to the empty chair in the bathroom. "We have a hair emergency. We need to do something with yours."

I notice she's already plugged a curling iron into the wall. The counter is full of enough hair products to fill a hair salon.

This is going to be a longer day than I planned.

A quick hour later, my hair's now in perfect curls. The curls feel bouncy and frame my face perfectly. I spot the time. It's getting close to three.

Ben brings my phone into the bathroom, "Chuck texted."

I look down and read, *"Happy Prom day! What time are you leaving? I'd love to take some pictures. I'm at the store all day. Have you thought about our conversation?"*

I respond, *"We're probably leaving at five. Come down whenever you can."*

"What did he want, Lucy?" Sarah asks.

"To take pictures with me before we leave."

"That's so sweet! I've always liked him. Glad to know he's stepped up with your mom gone and everything. Have you talked to her at all?"

"Yeah, this morning. She was asking me for clothes for her court case. Can you believe that? I hung up on her because I can't deal with her shit anymore."

Lauren laughs, "She asked for clothes? Are you serious? She's too much."

"She is, but I'm not going to worry about it. Today is for us. You two are the best friends that anyone could ever hope for."

"Agreed." Sarah says.

"Yep, you two are the sisters I always wanted. Hold on, I need to get something in the kitchen!" Lauren says.

Sarah says, "Do you know what she's getting?"

I shrug my shoulders and say, "No clue."

Lauren shouts, "Sarah, Lucy, get in here. I have a surprise."

We go into the kitchen where she's poured apple cider into three glasses. "This is so beautiful." Sarah says.

"I figured we should drink the cider out here. I'm not drinking cider anywhere near to the toilet!"

"Oh, Lauren. Gotta love her," Sarah says.

"No other way. She'll keep us young."

"Are you guys ready to cheers to your friendship and prom?" Maria asks.

"Yes, I'm so ready. I feel like I've been waiting for this day for a long time."

The sparkling goodness fills our glasses and I realize Ben isn't here to celebrate with us. This moment is for friends of a lifetime and not my relationship with him. I don't deserve such good friends. I owe everything to them.

"To our friendship. I love you both," Sarah says and we raise our glasses to the sky.

The glasses clink in unison and the cider reaches my lips. The apples taste so sweet and the bubbles tickle my throat. It reaches my stomach like bliss and friendship.

Before drinking more of this blissed-out beverage, Ben walks into the kitchen."Hey, everyone, question here. What time's dinner tonight? I thought it was six o'clock, right?"

I think to myself for a minute. I remember Lauren mentioning a time earlier, but I was probably daydreaming or not paying much attention.

Lauren replies, "Our reservation's at 6:30. But Luis and Sarah's date, Elizabeth, are coming over at 5:45 to take pictures. Good for you, Ben. I didn't know you were so excited about tonight."

Ben looks at the floor and crosses his toes. "Well, I hate to be the one to tell you this, but it's already 5:15—"

Lauren zooms out of the kitchen and beelines for the bathroom. Well, I'm guessing the bathroom, based on how fast the time has flown by today.

We walk into the bathroom and notice Luis is on speakerphone with a panicked Lauren.

His sweet, calming voice says, "Babe, it's okay. You'll look perfect no matter what. Try not to stress."

Lauren, who's nearly in tears, whines, "You're supposed to say nice things like that since you're my boyfriend. I'm going to look so ugly compared to everyone else."

I run into the kitchen. "Maria, we have an emergency and need your help. I know you're a little hungover, but you're our only hope."

She looks slightly confused, yet still follows me into the bathroom. Lauren isn't on the phone with Luis anymore and has her head in her hands. She's sobbing and her red hair muffles her cries. She looks like a red blob that's shaking uncontrollably.

"We need to fix this emergency of Lauren only having a limited time to get ready by doing her makeup and hair as quickly as possible. But, not too quick. I want her to look as good as she made Sarah and I. Does that make sense?"

Maria's close to being an expert because her makeup usually looks flawless. Today is an exception since she spent the night watching comic book adventures. Lauren looks up. "Wait, did you guys think of Maria to do my makeup?"

Sarah scrambles for words. "We... uh—"

Before Sarah finishes her sentence, I cut her off. "Well, Maria's as close as we're going to get with a professional of eyeshadow and stuff. I don't know enough to help you."

Sarah nods. "Yeah, I wouldn't be much help either."

Before we say anything else, Lauren kicks us out of the bathroom. "Okay, it's a little too crowded in here. You guys can do something for me. Grab all the glitter-filled eyeshadow you can find out there. And lipstick!"

We follow her orders, I scop up a lot of mascaras, then notice purple, green, and blue eyeshadow, but I question if Lauren even wants to wear any of those colors. They're truly hideous and I'm almost one hundred percent sure she wouldn't wear them.

Sarah finds some pretty brown eyeshadow and pink lipstick that will probably look great with Lauren's marshmallow-looking skin. We drop the treasures off on the bathroom counter while Maria sings along to some playlist Lauren made and we head into my room.

Sarah says, "So, how are we going to keep ourselves busy? We have a little bit before everyone else arrives and we have to take stupid photos."

"Yeah, I'm just ready for everyone to get here so the night can get started. Speaking of which, what time's Elizabeth getting here?"

Sarah's face is blinded by her phone and she's texting up a storm. I usually hate it when people are on their phone like this, but the smile on her face makes up for it.

I tap my foot. "Hello, Sarah? Anyone home?"

She looks up. "Sorry. What were you saying? I blanked out for a second."

I roll my eyes because sometimes I don't understand the obsession with phones. Then I realized without my phone there wouldn't be any cute cat videos for me to watch or the ability to talk to friends. I guess it's a tradeoff. "What time's Elizabeth getting here?"

"Probably in about thirty minutes. Look at this picture she just sent me. Doesn't she look beautiful?"

I look at the photo of Elizabeth. Her dark-black hair provides a wonderful contrast to her shiny blue eyes. Elizabeth is beautiful and I hope she's as nice as she looks. I've never gotten to know her except for a few hellos and waves.

"Yes, she looks great. I'm so excited to get to know her tonight. She better not be crazy. You know I have your back, right?"

"Yes, I'm excited, but I'm also nervous. What if she ends up not wanting to go with me anymore? Or leaves me on the dance floor alone? What will I do then?"

"I mean this in the nicest way possible, Sarah. But your anxiety's totally lying to you right now. You're going to be fine; if it doesn't work out, it's her loss anyway. You are a prize. Don't settle for someone who doesn't respect the amazing person you are."

"Yeah. You're right." But she sounds like someone that dropped their ice cream cone.

"Why do you sound so sad? Is there something you're not telling me?"

"No, I'm just stuck. Stuck in this place where I'm so jealous of you. I mean, you have such a perfect life with Ben. Then there's me just sitting here like a loser freaking out about my date. What the fuck's wrong with me?"

I shake Sarah and look her in the eyes. "Listen, Ben and I are definitely cute, but we have problems too. Sometimes he forgets to put deodorant on or I get angry for no reason a lot of the time. Life never slows down, we just get better at it."

"But, what if I want it to slow down? What if I don't get my happily ever after?"

I wish I could have all the answers for her. I wish I could wave a wand and have everything fall into place. But, maybe Tiffany was right.

"Tiffany taught me something important recently. Turn those if's into when's!"

"You're right, Lucy. Thank you."

"If this stuff with my mom has taught me anything, it's that we're all just doing the best we can. Even if it means we murder people at the grocery store. Maybe that's not a good example. Don't do that. I don't want to have to visit you in jail, too."

"You're so ridiculous, Lucy. But you're also an amazing friend. I'm not going to murder anyone. Well, at least any time soon. I need to calm down. Let's get dressed and forget all the bullshit for a while."

We zip each other's dresses, I put my sneakers on, she slides her gorgeous black flats on, and we walk out to the living room.

Lauren's makeup is done and her hair looks nearly fully curled. I walk into the kitchen while Sarah hangs out with Lauren to keep her company. I find Tiffany crying with a silver spoonful of smooth peanut butter in her mouth.

I stop in my tracks and go up to her.

"What's wrong? Why are you crying?"

She rubs her eyes and eats the rest of the peanut butter on the spoon. "I'm just thinking a lot about things, and it's left me in a black hole of emotion."

"If you don't mind me asking, what's bringing you down? Thinking a lot makes me sad too, but lately, I've been pushing my emotions away because I'm fearful they'll take over. If they succeed and take over, I won't be able to function at all or even get out of bed."

"I understand completely what you are talking about. We're definitely related because I've done the same thing since I got here. I saw the picture of your mom on the fridge and the emotions just flew out of me like a bat in a cave."

"Well, the stuff with my mom was impacting me a lot for a while. But, I'm beginning to look back on my life with her. It's starting to feel better imagining a life without her. I feel bad about it since she's, my mom. But, I'm just going with it. Does that make sense?"

"Yes, Lucy, it makes perfect sense. I still can't help feeling like I screwed up at being an older sister. Maybe if I'd visited you both more, maybe she would've felt better and wouldn't have killed Raymond."

She pauses and starts sobbing. I grab her hand.

"It's not your fault." I say.

She nods and continues, "She was probably lonely and could've needed more family around. I could've been that family, ya know? I doubt Raymond was nice to her. You wouldn't feel so damaged all the time because I'd make sure she never made you feel like garbage. I could've helped a lot.."

"Maybe that's true. Maybe it's not. We'll never know…"

Chuck pops out of nowhere, "Please don't beat yourself up about this, Tiffany. These last few weeks I've been tossing and turning about what I could have done to support Kelly. Despite my dad dying because of her, she still is a human being.. But, my sponsor helped me realize that the actions of others have nothing to do with me. Nothing is ever personal. Kelly definitely has some issues, but it doesn't mean I can fix her. Ya know?"

"What's a sponsor?" I ask.

"Well, in these Alcoholics Anonymous meetings, they have sponsors as support systems when you just need to talk to someone who understands. It's helping me. That and having sober friends."

A peace of mind and simultaneously anger washes over me like an ocean wave. Her actions have nothing to do with me and that within itself, feels like healing. I'm also frustrated that she is continuing to leave everyone around her feeling like there's something wrong with them. She's the most selfish person I've ever met.

Healing may be happening which is great. However, I'm tired of learning all of these life lessons. I just want to be a *normal* kid. One without bipolar. One without a mom in jail. One without panic attacks.

Does that make me too demanding?

Maria comes into the kitchen. "I now present to you the lovely Lauren! Lauren has a perfect face and look at that hair, folks!"

Lauren walks across the kitchen floor like it's a runway, flips her luxurious locks and bats her long eyelashes. "What do you ladies think? Good enough for tonight?"

I nod and give her a thumbs-up. "You look amazing. Luis is going to be so lucky to have you on his arm tonight. Great job, Maria!"

Lauren laughs. "I didn't put this on for him. He just gets to enjoy all this while I know I'm looking fine."

Maria high-fives Lauren. "You look beautiful, Lauren! Go get dressed. Luis be here soon!"

Lauren looks at the time on her phone. "Shit! Everyone will be here in less than five minutes."

Tiffany, Maria, and I stay in the kitchen. My guess is Ben's still getting ready. Sarah's still stuck on her phone like glue.

Maria looks at Tiffany. "What's up with you? You seem off."

Tiffany puts her hands up in the air. "I don't know. I was feeling fine, eating some peanut butter, and then I broke down. I just wish we could've been there for Lucy more and then maybe Kelly wouldn't have killed that dude. I mean, maybe his life would've been spared if one Christmas could've been with all of us. She was probably lonely and now she's in jail. It feels like my fault."

Maria grabs Tiffany's hand. "Babe, I mean in the nicest way possible, but you don't hold that much power. Your sister was a huge asshole. She's not worth you being sad about at all."

Tiffany exhales and unclenches her fists. "I don't know about you sometimes. You can take me out of my darkest moments and still make me laugh."

The doorbell rings. Perfect timing. Their love fests are growing gross.

Luis and Elizabeth look like a dream.

We've taken enough pictures to fill at least five photo albums. My cheeks are in so much pain from smiling and silly faces, I feel like I've been posing for a red-carpet premiere. Ben looks cute in his T-rex tie and seems a lot happier being around someone who isn't female. Luis is a lifesaver. I owe him big time.

I overhear him say, "Yeah, dude, *Moons for Millions* is for sure my favorite anime movie."

Luis replies, "You'll have to show me that one. I've only ever seen *Warp Mutant Drivers*, but I enjoyed it. Let's try and watch one after tonight's over."

"Man, I'm so glad you'll watch those with me. Lucy finds anime super boring. I don't know why I never thought of us being friends before. You're pretty awesome." Ben has a huge smile.

Before I respond with a joke since my head's full of so many,

Lauren says, "All right, everyone, it's time to go! We need to make it to dinner on time!"

Chuck pops out of nowhere and the bags under his eyes seem to be getting darker. "Lucy, stay there! I want a picture with you!"

Lauren says, "Are you serious, dude? Make it quick. We have to get to dinner."

I put my arm around Chuck and actually smile for the photo. Not the fake stuff that just happened.

We wave goodbye and I grab the lanyard for the black sedan. We rush to meet up with everyone. We decided that a limo was way too expensive. So, all the couples take separate cars to the restaurant and I'm ready to eat. I feel like I haven't eaten all day.

I open the glove box to look for snacks. My mom gets hungry every few hours like I do. The light turns on to display everything that's on the inside. There's a crinkled pack of silver Golden Gaucho cigarettes and two packs of gummy worms. I put a yellow and green sugar-crusted worm in my mouth. So gross. This must be what fishing bait tastes like.

Ben looks over at me for a second. "Whatcha eating over there, McBride? Care to share?"

My mouth's full. As much as I hate the taste of them, I can't stop.

I say, "I found some gummy worms. Don't judge me! It was the only thing to eat in this stupid car. Now, I can't stop. Take them away from me!"

"You're eating gummy worms? I've been trying to get you to eat those for so long! Give me some. I'm starving. What are you going to get for dinner? I want spaghetti and meatballs."

We get to the restaurant and Lauren goes up to the waitress. "Lauren, party of 6." she says.

CHAPTER EIGHTEEN

The waitress scans the computer looking for our reservation.

"Sorry, I'm not seeing you on the list for tonight. Could it be under a different name?"

"Luis, maybe?"

"No, we're still not coming up with anything. Sorry."

"Well, if we don't have a reservation, how long would we have to wait?"

"I want to say two hours at the very least. It looks like everyone at your school had the right idea of where to eat before Prom. Guess you're going to have to come back another day."

"Wow, thanks a lot. You just ruined our entire night!" Lauren says while storming off.

I go up to the waitress and say, "Sorry. She's a little bit dramatic sometimes."

She rolls her eyes, "I'll say. Hope to see you guys again soon."

I head to the parking lot where Luis is attempting to calm Lauren down. "Babe, it's just a restaurant. We'll figure something out. Don't worry."

I struggle with thinking of another restaurant we can go to until it hits me, The Holy Cow with Patty! "How about the Holy Cow, Lauren? You loved your food last time."

Sarah says, "That's a great idea, Lucy. I told you all about Elizabeth and it's when Ben asked you to Prom! We can end where we started!"

Ben says, "I love this idea. Let's go."

Lauren says, "Fine. I guess that's the best we have. Dumb restaurant losing my reservation. I'm never going back!"

"Yeah, they suck. Let's go."

My stomach is going to eat itself, but luckily, we made it here in one piece.

We all pile into a booth and all I can think about is hoping that the Patty will come by as soon as possible with a menu. I sit next to Ben and across from Sarah. Sarah's anxiety about her and Elizabeth not getting along was totally wrong. I've never seen her smile so much.

I drink some of my ice-cold water and look at everyone at the table. What a good night. Especially since it's just beginning.

Patty in her usual cute self is our waitress. She must be amazing at her job because she never takes our orders.

Lauren says, "I'm so excited to dance. Are you all going to join me on the dance floor? I don't care if we're the only ones out there. I'm going to do it anyway and have all the great moves."

Elizabeth says, "I'm the best at Gangnam style, so I'll join you to show off my sweet dancing."

Ben says, "Luis and ladies, we're forgetting the most important dance move of all. I'll be doing it the whole night no matter what the song."

I roll my eyes because I know exactly where this is going. "Do not ask him what dance move. Just change the conversation and everything will be alright."

Luis, who looks genuinely intrigued, says, "What dance move are you talking about, brother? I want you to teach me!"

Ben glances around the table. "Two words—the robot. I know what you're all thinking. The dance move is so old and no one likes it. But

I'm here to tell you, it's the best dance move of all the time. I will gladly teach you, Luis."

Ben shows Luis how to do the robot. Lauren pulls out her phone and starts recording. I laugh so hard, my stomach hurts and my lungs gasp for air.

Patty comes up to our table with our food and notices the boys dancing. "Back in my day, people were into the Mashed Potato, but I think that robot stuff you're doing has them beat. Are you guys going to a dance tonight?"

Elizabeth clears her throat and stops laughing. "Yes, it's our Prom night. We're just practicing what we're going to do when we get there later."

"Oh, okay, that makes sense. I was wondering why you kids were dressed so fancy. Who's hungry?"

Before I can check in with everyone who's attacking their food, my phone vibrates. I look at the message. *"Watch your back, McBride."*

I check behind me just in case someone is actually there. I only see tables full of old people talking to each other. No one seems to be on their phone in the entire restaurant.

"Guys, did one of you text me from a private number to be funny?"

Luis swallows his food and leaves marinara sauce on the corners of his mouth. "Lucy, I know for sure you don't have my number, but I promise, it wasn't me."

Sarah looks up from her moss-green salad. "What are you talking about?"

I pass my phone around the table. "I just got the creepiest text. I don't recognize the number or understand why anyone would send me that."

The hair on the back of my neck and arms stand straight up like blades of grass. Am I next? Will I be the next murder in this small town?

Every person at the table has finished their meal. But as much as I wanted to finish my pancakes, fear lingers in the pit of my stomach. My body feels unsteady. My hands feel like there are ants swimming in them and my brain feels like it's in a blender.

Who could it have been? Is it someone taking revenge on Raymond?

I'm terrified.

While everyone figures out how to divide the check, I head to the bathroom. The feeling of panic in every step is nothing new. The lights and walls in this restaurant seem familiar. A headache lingers and the walls make me feel boxed in.

I run into the stall as quickly as I can to center my body. The cold toilet feels good on my skin and my feet feel planted to the floor. I close my eyes and picture roots coming out of my feet. I'm a big anxious tree. A tree that wants to go home and cuddle Snowball.

Before I fall into a whirlpool of despair, I hear a knock on the bathroom stall.

Sarah says, "Lucy, do you need us to come in there? You've been in there for a while."

Lauren adds, "We're going to have so much fun tonight. Let's get it started! Everyone else doesn't matter. Just the three of us do."

Now I think I hear Elizabeth's voice. Well, at least I hope it's her.

"You mean four, right Lauren?"

"Yes, Elizabeth, you're right. C'mon, Lucy."

"Sorry. I feel down. I'm trying not to let my depression win, but it definitely is right now. I don't understand why someone would send me such a scary text."

Elizabeth says, "Lucy, I know you're feeling shitty, but I hope you come out soon. Prom's not my thing, but when Sarah asked, I had to say yes. I have depression and honestly almost forgot to take my pills today. I hope I can get to know you better. We can even be depression buddies!"

Depression buddies. I like the sound of that. I've always wanted to have someone who could relate to my mental health. Lauren plays a lot of sports, so I don't always think her brain understands what depression feels like. Sarah likes to tie-dye and make pottery, so maybe her depression just comes out in the form of bright colors. I don't know Elizabeth's hobbies, but I'm hoping she'll become a great friend.

I stand from the porcelain seat, open the stall door, and walk into the arms of my amazing friends. The weight of their bodies almost stabilizes me. The world doesn't feel dizzy and fall apart-y anymore. A part of me wishes I could splash water on my face because that always makes me feel better. Water on the face isn't such a good idea with all this makeup. I wouldn't even know how to start reapplying it.

As we walk through the bathroom doors together, I feel unstoppable with these amazing women by my side. I'm going to be okay. I need to keep telling myself that.

As soon as we get back to the table, Ben gives me a huge hug. "Glad you're doing better."

"Me, too."

"The check's taken care of. Now, let's get the heck out of here and have some fun!" Luis says while grabbing Lauren's hand.

"See you guys soon!" Elizabeth says while she gets in Sarah's car. It's comforting to know we aren't parked next to some weirdo who could hit our cars or something.

"I need to talk to you about something, Ben. There's something I haven't talked to you about yet and figured you deserve to know."

"Oh, god. What is it? Are you breaking up with me? I knew it. You've been going through a lot lately and I mean I bet you want to process it…"

"Ben! Shut up! I'm not breaking up with you. It's about the store."

"Oh, phew. Warning next time! You know I don't do well with surprises." I feel bad. Sometimes, I forget all about Ben's triggers. Especially lately with everything going on. I have been in full survival mode.

"Okay, so you remember that day that Chuck had me come into his office? Well, he asked me if I want to run Smiles with him. I don't know what to do."

"I knew he was going to ask you. I was just waiting for when. What do you want to do?"

"Honestly, I just want to go to Seattle. Does that make me a bad person? I know Chuck is relying on me, but my heart isn't in it."

"Then tell him that. He may be upset at first, but he wants you to be happy. The sooner you tell him, the better. It's not like he's going to hate you or something."

The idea of Chuck killing me makes me laugh. How ironic would that be? It would have to be on aisle three, too.

"Well, what do you want to do? I mean you're part of any future I have."

"In all seriousness, Lucy, I wish I could just snap my fingers and be in Seattle already. I'm ready for prom to be over and just forget all this stupid shit."

"Are we fooling ourselves, do you think? Like what if we get to Seattle and realize we hate it? What do we do then?"

"Stop worrying about things you can't control. If we hate Seattle, we can move. It wouldn't be the end of the world. I have heard Texas is nice, too. Way cheaper than moving to California or something. One-bedroom apartments are like five thousand dollars there and that's considered cheap!"

"Texas? Seriously? I'm not about to move somewhere hotter and filled with even more cowboy boots and racists. Don't even get me started on California. I don't want to move somewhere full of surfers everywhere. I've heard good things about Santa Barbara, though."

"Santa Barbara definitely has a nice ring to it, but I think Seattle's the best choice for us."

I exhale for what feels like the first time all night. "Well, Benny, I guess we're doing this. No looking back now."

"Nope, we can't look back. Just move forward. We need to focus on right now and our night together. It's not like Seattle is going anywhere. Pretty sure there's no zombie apocalypse or alien invasion that's going to attack the city any time soon. Just breathe."

"What about aliens? They could totally destroy Seattle. I can just see it now, a huge spaceship destroying all the coffee shops and bookstores! What are people going to do without their vanilla lattes and comic books?"

"Society as we know it would collapse! People can't live without their 6 AM coffee. We must prevent this. I know what we will fix it!"

"Don't you even dare!"

He parks the car and starts doing the robot again, "Do what, Lucy?"

A smile is glued to my face and I kiss him on the lips.

"You're such a dork. Now, let's go!"

As I step out and straighten my dress in the back, I feel full of anxiety. I don't want to make conversation with anyone and hope no one causes any drama. I've had enough drama and confusion about life this month to last me a lifetime. Ben grabs my hand. "We got this."

He's right. I'm good. I got this.

Sarah turns around, while she leads the pack of us, she holds Elizabeth's hand. "Dang, they made this gym actually look good."

I've been looking at my feet since we got here to make sure I don't trip in front of everyone. I tend to be clumsier when I'm at this degree of nervousness around people. While looking around, I notice yellow and blue Christmas lights lining the walls and gold balloons glittering the dance floor.

Everyone's smiling and looks excellent in their outfits. Some of the girls' dresses make them look like they're brides. Props to them. I'd definitely fall over in that poofy of a dress and high heels. The dresses remind me of the cake toppers on fancy baking shows. I see a lot of duck faces and groups of people huddling around each other with big smiles. Lauren and Luis drag the group of us to another room. Is there another prom I don't know about? A quieter one with better music?

Sadly, I'm wrong. They've dragged us to take professional photos. The backdrop is the Paris sky full of fake stars and the Eiffel Tower is all lit up. I see the words PARIS IN LOVE, which I guess is the theme. Better than a circus theme with dumb clowns or something stupid like that.

Ben and I stand in the typical pose. The one where a person grabs the other person around the waist and you both face the camera. I smile and the flash burns my eyes.

The camera guy with the collared blue shirt tells us, "Keep your eyes open this time! We want to make sure it's you we're looking at when they get printed!"

I open my eyes and have a forced smile on my face. I hope these photos turn out better than my body feels.

"You guys know what time it is?" Luis says.

"Show time!" I say.

Dancing can be fun if you forget how dumb you look. Beads of sweat drip down my forehead and I keep having to wipe them off. I hope they're not smudging my makeup. I don't want to look like my skin is shedding like a lizard.

Ben twirls me around and pulls me in closer. "You look so beautiful, Lucy. The sweat on your face makes you look like you're sparkling."

"Thanks, I guess? Is that a compliment?"

"Of course it is. You're my shiny galaxy. I love you."

"I love you, too. Thanks for convincing me to come.

Sarah grabs mine and Lauren's hand and the three of us dance together. We sing along to the Glitter Tooth song, "Stars in Your Eyes" the DJ's playing. This song used to be the one we'd belt out on repeat when we were younger. We used to think we were so cool, but now I know for sure that we, in fact, are. I have everything I could ever need in this exact moment, except for the tiramisu calling my name and my full bladder. The tiramisu sits on a table away from the dance floor, right next to a bowl full of bright blood-red punch.

"I need to go to the bathroom." I say to everyone before I explode.

Ben puts his thumb up in the air because the music's too loud for anyone to hear me anyway. I weave in and out of people dancing close to each other. The room is humid from all the body heat. It's gross.

I walk with my head down and go straight to the bathroom, so no one talks to me. The line's over ten people long. While standing around, I notice everyone's either texting, taking pictures with filters, or looking at their reflections in their compact mirrors. A few girls do have pretty dresses on, though. Someone even has on a leopard-print dress. I don't think I could ever be that fearless in my clothing choices, but she's definitely rocking it.

While I watch people and make up stories about them and their lives, I feel a tap on my shoulder. There goes me not talking to anyone.

I turn around and face my fate. "Hey. Aren't you that girl who's mom murdered someone?"

"Yeah...what about it?" I say sounding way more ruder than I anticipated. I hope they're not one of Rebecca's followers and are here to make fun of me.

"Well, I just wanted to introduce myself. My name is Blue. I moved here at the beginning of the school year."

"Cool, nice to meet you Blue. I'm Lucy. I like your outfit."

Blue's wearing a purple and green suit. They even have a cane that's covered in fake diamonds and a blue feather in their hat.

"Thanks so much. I love that you're wearing sneakers. Those are probably way more comfortable than heels."

"You have no idea." I say while I notice some girls cut in front of us. I want to say something, but I enjoy talking with Blue.

"So, the reason why I wanted to talk to you was because of something personal."

Were they the one that sent me the text to watch my back? Are they going to kill me in front of all of these people? That seems like a dumb thing to do in public, but people don't make sense.

"Okay…" I say while noticing the exit and figuring out the fastest way to get out of here.

"Well, my mom murdered my dad which is why I moved here. She went to jail and now my grandparents watch me. I wanted to tell you that I think you're brave for going back to school and everything. I know I hid away and didn't see anyone for a long time."

"Thanks so much. I appreciate that. I definitely am struggling to be here, but have to remind myself that it's my senior year and stuff. Better make it count or whatever."

"I'm so jealous. I'm only a junior and am so ready to get out of here."

"I feel you on that. I'm sorry if I was rude earlier. I wasn't trying to be. I just get nervous with this many people around."

"I get it. No need to explain. I'm lucky to be the only trans person at this whole town. It can be frustrating at times and I used to have panic attacks all the time from people spitting on me. But now, I realize they're all idiots and don't fucking matter."

A door to a bathroom opens. Before I run over to grab it, I say, "Nice meeting you Blue. Good luck with everything. I hope your senior year goes fast."

I run to the open stall, so no one steals it and sit down. On the back of the stall are school related yellow and blue posters that say CLASS OF 2021! A part of me has been ready for 2021 for as long as I can remember. This year's full of me turning eighteen and graduating. I picture everything getting a little bit easier simply because I don't know how much more I can handle. I'd like to think my twenties will be full of ice cream for dinner, lots of silly dancing, and doing whatever I want without anyone bothering me. What a life it will be.

I wash my hands in a quick lather and get out of the bathroom as soon as possible with the line just getting longer and longer. I hear the music rumbling so loud the water on the table looks like it's vibrating. I want to dance, however want dessert more. Everyone will understand. I mean, I didn't eat much of my dinner and now my stomach's rumbling.

As I walk over to the yellow and blue table, I hear Sarah's voice. She and Elizabeth are sitting at a table with and sweaty faces and plates full of tiramisu. Sarah's hair is back to being completely flat. The two of them are adorable.

I grab my dessert and sit next to them. "Where is everyone?"

"Oh, they're dancing out there in the beauty of the dance floor. You never told us Ben was such a good dancer. Best part of the night, Lucy," Elizabeth says with a huge grin.

"You're joking, right? That dude just knows the robot. Is he living a secret life?" I say with frosting on the edge of my mouth. My body gets a surge of energy from all the sugar.

I zigzag my way through the funky smells from the mob of people again. The lights shining above burn my eyes. Who thought it was a good idea to make these lights so bright?

CHAPTER NINETEEN

I spot Lauren and Luis making out. I want to ask them where Ben is but don't want to interrupt. I dart my eyes around and notice I'm the only one not coupled.

A girl in a black dress, who's in my math class, grabs my attention. "Hey, isn't that your boyfriend?" She points at Ben.

I nod. "Thank you."

Sure enough, she's right. I walk over, I notice Rebecca Gardner dancing in his general direction. Rebecca is wearing a white dress. No joke. She looks like one of those pop singers from the 90s. She is way too much. I'm going to try and ignore her.

I hug Ben from behind and whisper in his ear, "Hey, stranger, miss me?"

"May I have this dance?" he asks.

We dance around together and as much as I enjoy myself and surprisingly the music, Rebecca's still in direct view of us. No one pays attention to her except for a few people who look like they don't have dates. A part of me believes she's dancing on her own to get more attention. Honestly, I wouldn't put it past her.

She walks over to us. "Hey, McBride, want a picture? Stop looking at me. It's weird."

"I'm not even looking at you. Get out of here."

She gasps. "Oh, Lucy, just because I look better in my dress and my hair's prettier than yours doesn't mean you have to be jealous. I know I look great and everyone's looking at me. You don't have to tell me."

Before I can respond, Blue shows up out of nowhere.

They look Rebecca up and down. "Wow, how desperate are you? You don't need to talk to Lucy like that. She did nothing to you."

Rebecca stops dancing. "Excuse me, did someone ask you to talk? What are you anyway? A boy or a girl? You look hideous. I'm surprised anyone wanted to go to Prom with you to begin with."

Blue's eyes bug out. Their eyes look like flames are going to come out of them.

"Why does my gender matter so much to you? Don't you have someone else you can bother? My date is beautiful, unlike you, and at least I have one. Where's yours?"

"Actually, I do have a date. He went to get us some punch. Now, get out of my face. I was talking to Lucy. Don't make me have my boyfriend beat you up."

"Why would he beat me up? I'm asking a simple question, why are you treating Lucy like trash? She doesn't deserve that."

"You're so annoying. If you know Lucy so well, what's her phone number?"

I'm so confused. What does that have to do with anything?

"My phone number? That's so random. Wait, are you the one who texted me earlier?"

"Yeah and I meant it. Like I said earlier, you better watch your back. You think you're so cool with your friends and yellow dress, McBride. But you're not. Bet you didn't think you'd be getting in a fight tonight, huh?"

Rebecca's hands ball into fists like she's ready to hit me in the face. Everyone has their phones out ready to record it. With perfect timing, Julio walks over with the punch, but he accidentally trips right when he reaches us and spills the bright punch all over Rebecca's white dress. Hah her dress! It's completely stained!

She yells, "Are you serious, babe? You're such an idiot!"

Julio runs after her with the empty cups in his hands. "Wait up! I want to help get the punch out."

Blue, Ben, and I all walk outside of the dance floor.

Blue says, "I hate that girl. I'm glad she didn't cause you any more trouble. I would've had no problem teaching her a lesson."

I don't know what to say except to go in for a hug. Someone who barely knows me actually stood up for me.

"Thank you so much. She's just a bully. I hate her."

Blue straightens their green tie. "Of course. I know you've been through enough the last few weeks. I don't want anything else happening to you."

Ben steps in. "Hi, I'm Ben. Thanks for that. Rebecca's such a bitch. What's your name? Are you in one of Lucy's classes?"

Blue puts their hand out and shakes Ben's. "I'm Blue. I met your girlfriend in the bathroom. I'm new to the school this year which is probably why you haven't seen me before. I wish I were graduating with you guys."

"Well, thanks. Also, I love your outfit! Are you supposed to be Agent Green from the Promises of Darkness?"

"Hell yeah, I am! You're the first person that got it all night! How did you know?"

"Of course I'd know. I watch *The Crazy Comic Corners* all the time. Collectors always talk about Agent Green. I'm surprised they haven't made a movie yet!"

"They are supposed to next year. Honestly, you never know with superhero movies. Sometimes they're popular and other times, people just hate them." Blue says while I notice a semicolon on their wrist.

"What's that? Are you into grammar or something?"

Ben nudges me, "Lucy! You don't just go around asking people about their tattoos."

Blue laughs, "No, ask away! Semicolons are a symbol in the world of mental health. Authors use them to join two thoughts together. On my body, it means that my story isn't over yet and there's so much more to come."

"I love that so much! I want to get one!" I say.

A girl in a beautiful purple dress comes up to us and says, "Blue! There you are. I've been looking everywhere. I want to dance!"

Blue winks and says, "Duty calls. See you later, Lucy."

As bad as it sounds, I'm glad Rebecca's dress got ruined. She's not a nice person and she shouldn't think her behavior towards me is okay. I may not always know how to stand up for myself, however, it still doesn't make it right. Especially since she's been treating me like shit for way too long.

Ben and I dance the rest of the night away. I don't even remember what songs the best were, but I do know this night was way better than I ever planned. The air's sweeter than the tiramisu and the uphill battle feels as if it's getting a little less unsteady.

The last song dwindles to a stop.

We three couples go our separate ways. I'm left with a state of euphoria that Arizona has never had. I guess dancing can do that to you.

I wish I could say today has been super productive. I wish I could tell you I drank a kale smoothie to stay healthy. But, I've done the opposite.

I woke up at eleven to texts from Lauren and Sarah telling me how much fun they had and hundreds of pictures. I also made brownies and watched a lot of cartoon movies, and just like the chocolate chips in the batter, I have melted into the couch. Relaxing feels nice, it put a necessary pause on my brain. Maria and Tiffany stopped by earlier, but they wanted to go look at wedding dresses. I'm way too tired to join them.

Chuck texted me early this morning saying, *"Donuts and chocolate milk today?"*

I haven't responded because I'm avoiding him. Avoiding our big conversation about the future. I know I should face my fears and everything, but I'd hate to let him down. Ben comes in for another brownie with his frozen almond milk, "So, when are you going in?"

"Going in where?" I say.

"The store, goober. Don't think you can get away with it, McBride. You have to tell him today. The longer you wait, the harder…"

"The harder it will be. I know. Before I leave, promise me something, okay?"

"Of course."

"Promise me that we'll look for places to stay when I come back."

"Pinky promise. I already have a few leads." he says while locking his with mine.

I put on an oversized shirt and a pair of gray leggings. My dress from last night is sprawled out on the bed. Snowball is curled up on my side of the bed and I just wish I could join her.

I need to push through.

I grab the keys for the car and head for the store. I'm going to have to come with a gift or something to help him not be too mad at me.

I print out a picture of me and him from last night. I find a funny mug for his desk. I also grab the most important items, the donuts and milk.

I go to the front and Blue is behind the register. Of course.

"Hey Lucy. What are you doing here?"

"Just buying some stuff for my dad. I have to tell him that I'm moving to Seattle after graduation and stuff. I'm nervous about it."

They scan my items and flash their wrist again. They catch me looking at it. "Remember what it means. Your story isn't over yet. Besides, it's your life anyway. Do what you want."

I notice a permanent marker by the receipt printer.

"Hey, can I use that marker?" I say.

"Of course."

I take it and draw a semicolon on my wrist. Maybe having this will remind me to keep believing in myself. Keep believing in a better future.

I pay for my stuff and cruise to the store.

The lights are already on and the parking lot is full. I mean it's Sunday. Why did I think anything different?

I grip the plastic bag of goodies and I make my way through the revolving doors, suddenly I'm confronted with Julio. I ignore eye contact with and avoid him like the plague.

"Lucy, can we talk?" he says.

I don't want to be nice to him, but it's a good distraction from having to find Chuck.

"What do you want? Here to make fun of me?"

"No, I don't want to make fun of you. I wanted to say sorry."

"Sorry? For what?" I'm so confused. Is he being genuine? Does he care about my feelings? This must be his evil twin or something.

"I'm sorry for last night. I shouldn't have given Rebecca your phone number. I shouldn't have let her be so mean."

"Don't worry about it. It's not your fault she's a bitch."

I don't know what's come over me. I actually feel bad for Julio. I know what it feels like to love someone who's terrible. I mean mom was family and all that, but I bet Julio has low confidence because of it. No one deserves to feel like that.

"Well, I broke up with her and I made you something."

"What?"

He leads his way through the grocery store. I wave to people I know and we end up on aisle three.

I close my eyes out of fear of being trapped in a mist of memories. A mist of blood everywhere, stained apples, and a dead body.

"Lucy, open your eyes." Julio says.

I begin to squint and then fully open my eyes. Next to the prices of the apples, Julio has written, "In memory of Raymond Williams. A friend to all."

"Have you shown this to Chuck?"

"No, not yet. Should I go find him?"

"Umm, yes! Of course! This is so sweet, Julio." I say while going in for a hug.

Julio runs to the front of the store, "Chuck, you are wanted on aisle three."

Chuck finds us, full of nothing but smiles. Something I never thought would happen. Especially with Julio next to me.

"Lucy, when did you get here?"

"A little bit ago, but look at what Julio did!"

Julio says, "Well, I shouldn't take all the credit. My mom helped, too." Rosa is talking to a customer, yet I still say thank you.

Chuck says, "I don't even know what to say. This is so nice."

"You're welcome, sir. If you don't mind, I have to go back to work. See you later, Lucy."

"See you later, Julio." I turn to Chuck. "Can we go to your office? We should talk."

"Thought you'd never ask."

Chuck shields me from most of the customers in the store. There are a few that notice me and I just wave. It's nice knowing people care about me though talking to Chuck is my priority.

He shuts the door and says, "Did you bring the milk and donuts? I've been craving them all morning."

I throw them to him and he devours them like a lion with their prey.

"Dude, this isn't going to be easy for me to say. Please don't get mad at me…" I say while my voice breaks.

"I'm not going to get mad…"

"I need to move out of Arizona. I mean, I just have so many memories of mom and everything. I just need somewhere that's—not— here. I feel bad, but I know you understand. I just don't want to let you down since I'm your only family and stuff."

"You're not letting me down. Trust me. I figured that you were going to say no, so I thought of another plan."

"Another plan? You're not mad at me?"

"No, I'm not mad. A little disappointed, but I totally get it."

"That still doesn't answer my question, what's your plan?" I say while getting impatient.

"I'm making Rosa my assistant manager. She's going to own the store with me! It made the most sense. My dad loved her and she gives 100% every day. What do you think?"

I love this idea! I wish I could just go hug Rosa right now. She saved the store. She saved me. Most importantly, she saved Chuck.

"I think this is the smartest idea you've ever had! I need to hug Rosa, but one more thing. Close your eyes."

Chuck closes his eyes while I pull out his presents. I printed out a picture of us from last night for his desk. I also got him a mug that says, 'World's Okayest Dad."

I set them in front of him and say, "Okay, open."

He opens his eyes and is immediately drawn to the picture of us. "I love this picture, Lucy! I'm keeping it forever. This mug is perfect and I'm going to put my coffee in it every morning. Without any creamer."

I scrunch up my face at the idea of black coffee. "Do you like them?"

"I love them, my daughter. I love you and am proud of all you're becoming."

"I love you too, dad." Then my eyes get wet.

I look down at my wrist and the semicolon is smudged. But if you look close enough, you can see that it's still there.

My new adventure is on the horizon; my story is just beginning.

ACKNOWLEDGMENTS

My biggest thank you is to the readers. This book has been in progress since 2018. While writing this, I have spent more than I'd like to admit on pens, journals, and have had many sleepless nights. Despite the immense doubt and imposter syndrome, I knew I had to keep going. Thanks for making this a reality.

To Dad, Mom, Ryan, and Cameron: my first teachers. I love you all and thank you for everything you've done for me. You all are such a big inspiration to me.

To uncle Mike, thank you for all the books you got me for Christmas over the years. My love of reading inspired the love for words I have now. It led to writing this story. I love you!

To my O'Halloran family, I love you all. Thanks for everything.

To the Ohlen family, I love you and thanks for making me part of the family since day 1.

To Lake County and all of the amazing people I've met there, I love you and your resiliency has been one of the greatest gifts of my life.

To Madi and Travis: Thank you for letting me ramble about this book constantly and always taking time to make sure I was living and not just writing.

To the wonderful writers at the Santa Barbara Writers Conference, I don't even know where to begin. You all have taught me so much about being a writer and showing up for life. This book wouldn't be here without you.

To Jecoe Firmalan, thank you for your wonderful art for the cover. You were such an amazing partner in this and always listening to my needs. I'm indebted to you.

To Lauren, thank you for always believing in my writing and being one of the first people to acknowledge my talent. I will appreciate your faith in me forever. I love you.

To Sarah, ever since I met you at Charlie Browns, I knew you'd be a lifelong friend. I love you.

To K and M, my oldest friends. Thank you for being there for me since we were 3; can't wait for the next 103! I love you both.

To all of the friends I have made in other countries, Lake County, San Jose, college, a job, and the ones that were brought to me through fate, thank you. The joys I have had with you has kept me going and I'm grateful for each and every one with you.

To Fuzzykins, the real Snowball. Thank you for your late night cuddles and purrs. You are the greatest kitty ever and thanks for always being so empathetic.

To JoJo, I love you. Thanks for always listening even when I was erratic and thought no one would want to read this. Your support with buying me pens with LEDs and a red light by my bedside don't go unnoticed. Your support is so invaluable and one of my greatest gifts.

To grandpa, I miss you every day. Hope you're exploring the cosmos and other worlds. Wish you were still here, but I know you're still with me.

To anyone who has felt like Lucy, I love you. You are not alone. Your mental health doesn't define you. Your brain will lie to you; you are so loved. Don't doubt your worth. The world is yours.

ABOUT THE AUTHOR

Jordan O'Halloran is a YA author addicted to caffeine and the smell of books. She lives in Lake County. California with her partner, cat, and roommate. *Clean Up on Aisle Three* is her first book and she is definitely eager to publish more. When not writing, you can find her painting, being around nature, eating cheese, and taking naps. To continue following her journey, you can find her as *Jordanjotsjoy* on Instagram, Twitter, and Facebook.